THE WHITI KILLII

By Simon McCleave

A DI Ruth Hunter Crime Thriller
Book 6

Your FREE book is waiting for you now

Get your FREE copy of the prequel to
the DI Ruth Hunter Series NOW
at www.simonmccleave.com[1]
and join my VIP Email Club

For the fairy godmothers,
Kristin and Nyree

CHAPTER 1

EVEN THOUGH IT WAS a cold, frosty Sunday morning in early September, Abu Habib was sweating. The safety goggles he was wearing had steamed up, and he blinked as a bead of sweat stung his left eye. As he moved the Silverline soldering iron across to the square circuit board, his hand was shaking a little. He had been up all night, and a mixture of coffee, energy drinks and steely determination were the only things keeping him awake. But the combination made him jittery.

Dabbing gently at some solder, he saw it melt into a small globule of molten liquid. The metallic waft of burning floated into his nostrils; he was getting used to it. Using tweezers, Abu took the stripped end of the blue electrical wire and placed it into the liquid before it cooled. Once attached, it would create an electrical circuit, controlled by the simple push of a button.

Perfect, he thought, taking pride in how skilful he had become at this type of construction.

Outside, the yellow trams that dissected Manchester trundled in the distance, rumbling along their tracks. It was still early and the residents of Didsbury were asleep. It felt a long way from Abu's home town of Hemel Hempstead in the affluent county of Hertfordshire. The rustling noise of autumnal leaves came from the side passage, where the window was open. The sound was redolent of his childhood, and it made Abu sad to think about his family. He didn't know what would happen that evening, but he was struck by the thought that he might never see them again. And it scared him. He knew it shouldn't. He knew that he was safe in the hands of Allah. However, he felt the constant tussle between what he knew was spiritually true, and his more human gut instinct.

Pushing the goggles up, Abu wiped his sweaty brow and face with his sleeve, pushing aside the uncomfortable thoughts as he did so. The dark brown knitted kufi, which covered his virtually-bald head, wasn't helping to keep him cool.

His eyes flitted around the work surface. Electrical circuit boards, wires, pliers and the trigger button. Abu hadn't worked this intensely since he had gained a first-class honours degree in chemistry from Leeds University. Back then, his plan was to become a chemical engineer. He wanted to use his knowledge to help find viable sources of renewable energy and alternative carbon sources for clean fuel production. He was idealistic. He wanted to help save the planet. And his parents were so proud of what he had done with his life.

A decade later, Abu's life couldn't have been more different. His mother would now be horrified if she could see what he was doing today. Saving the planet wasn't part of his plan anymore.

Today, Abu Habib was building a bomb. An acetone peroxide-based nail and ball-bearing bomb. And that evening, he was going to detonate it at Manchester City's Etihad Stadium.

Swigging from his energy drink, Abu sat back to survey his work. He heard someone coming down the stairs. A young man in his twenties walked in and gave him a nod. Medhi Brahimi was an activist from the *Groupe Islamique Armé*, an extreme Algerian terror group. He had said very little since his arrival from North Africa a week ago. The only things Abu knew about Medhi were that he liked to read and smoke a bit of weed.

'*As-salamu alaykum,*' Abu said with a slight movement of his head. *Peace be upon you.*

Medhi nodded his head in response. '*Wa alaykum s-salaam,*' he mumbled, as he filled the kettle and put it on to boil. That was the other thing about Medhi; he liked mint tea with lots of sugar. He seemed to drink gallons of it.

Abu took a deep breath and looked again at the components laid out in front of him. There was at least another three hours' work before the bomb would be ready. He had been taught how to make the device by a member of the ISIS Battar Brigade who had flown in from Libya to help with the plot. Martyrdom in the name of Allah. A symbolic act that would send shock waves through the Western world.

There was a metallic clang from outside. Abu looked over at the window and then over to Medhi.

What was that?

He had kept the ground-floor window open to help with the acrid fumes that came from his soldering.

Abu froze and listened intently. His pulse quickened a little.

Then another noise.

Is this my imagination, or is something – or someone – moving outside?

Continual vigilance, verging on paranoia, was Abu's default setting. His life had become a complex web of lies and secrecy. False names, clandestine trips, and the continual feeling that he was being watched. In fact, he was certain that he was under the surveillance of MI5, Special Branch, and the Greater Manchester Police Counterterrorism Unit. He had seen the telltale signs in recent weeks. The woman carrying two bags of shopping, as though this was the perfect disguise, looking vacantly into the window of a record shop in central Manchester. The jogger with the large headphones, who had finished his run but seemed to have nowhere in particular to go. In Abu's experience, coppers looked like coppers no matter how well they'd disguised themselves. They thought they were cleverer than him – but he was, in fact, always one step ahead.

The previous evening he had bought two burner pay-as-you-go mobile phones from the supermarket - with cash, so that they were untraceable. He had shaved off his long beard, donned a pair of clear-lensed glasses, a black hoodie, and trackies instead of his Islamic prayer robe. As the leader of several Manchester terrorist cells, Abu was notorious but also highly respected in the circles that he now moved in.

The tense silence continued. Abu rose cautiously from his chair.

Then came a distinctive shuffle from outside.

Abu shot Medhi a look of concern. He gestured outside.

That's the sound of boots, isn't it?

Medhi tiptoed across the room, and then froze as he listened.

Moving to the window, Abu leant flat against the wall. His chest was rising faster as his breath quickened.

Glancing out of the open window, Abu couldn't see anything. A false alarm? There had been plenty of those before. Last time it was a bloody cat.

But then he saw something. The black shape of a helmet from behind a neighbour's wall. Then it disappeared. It was only a glimpse, but Abu knew exactly what was going to happen.

Shit. Armed officers! They were being raided.

His adrenaline skyrocketed. They needed to move swiftly. Destroy the evidence and escape.

Abu nodded to Mehdi to confirm their worst fears. He reached for the two-litre bottle of petrol they kept for this eventuality. Putting all documents and a laptop onto the table, he sloshed the petrol over them. He struck a match and tossed it. Within a second, the table was engulfed in orange flames.

We need to get out of here.

Medhi shoved the bomb-making ingredients into a rucksack, which he swung onto his back. The explosives weren't primed yet, but he didn't want to take his chance in a house fire with a ten-kilo bomb on his back.

They raced through the ground floor in total silence.

Abu reached the back door and crouched beside it. His heart was now thumping in his chest. He took a deep breath to steady himself.

They would come smashing through the front door any second now.

'Ready?' Abu whispered to Medhi, who looked terrified. The young man nodded, but his eyes moved uncontrollably with fear.

Preparing himself, Abu clasped the handle of the door and turned it slowly. He eased it open by about an inch. There was movement in the alleyway behind the house. More armed officers.

They were everywhere.

However, Abu and Medhi had no intention of going over the back wall. They had planned their escape route meticulously for just such an eventuality.

Right, here goes.

With a surge of adrenaline, Abu dashed out of the door. He ran to the neighbour's waist-high wall and vaulted it. Medhi followed.

'Armed police! Don't move!' shouted a voice.

They won't shoot us in the back.

Abu and Medhi were already sprinting across the neighbour's untidy garden. They jumped the wooden fence on the other side. A dog barked at them.

There was more shouting. Two armed police officers chased them.

'Oi! Police! Stay where you are!'

Gasping for breath, Abu and Medhi thundered across garden after garden, climbing and jumping fences as they went. Their movements were fast and precise.

Suddenly, a deafening thundering came from overhead.

A police helicopter loomed over them, the wind from its blades swirling leaves into the air.

Shit! This is not good. No time to stop.

Another fence. Another garden.

Glancing behind, Abu could see the officers were about fifty yards away. He pumped his arms as his lungs burned with the effort.

'Come on!' Abu barked at Medhi.

They were getting close to the next stage of their escape plan.

Another fence. Kids playing in a garden. A scream of terror.

Weaving right, Abu saw the high brick wall which backed onto the Didsbury Industrial Estate.

Bingo!

Medhi gave him a boost, and Abu got to the top. He reached down and pulled Medhi up.

They dropped down the other side.

The air was filled with the noise of the circling helicopter, police sirens, and shouting.

Sprinting at full pelt, Abu and Medhi disappeared into the industrial estate and out of sight.

CHAPTER 2

THE AUTUMN HAD ARRIVED with an imperceptibly slow grace. Sitting on her patio with a cigarette, coffee, and woollen blanket, Detective Inspector Ruth Hunter looked skywards as the tall trees of her garden shivered before casting down their cherry-coloured leaves like confetti. The air had an earthiness unique to the season.

Dragging the last half-inch of her ciggie, Ruth blew the bluish smoke up and watched as the autumnal wind grabbed and whisked it away. She blinked and rubbed her tired eyes. To say that she was having trouble sleeping in recent days was an understatement. As her dad would have once said, she was 'cream-crackered'.

Ruth opened her eyes as the sound of movement from the road caught her attention. She lived in the picturesque village of Bangor-on-Dee in North Wales. Checking her watch, she could see that it was approaching eleven o'clock. People from the village would be making their way to the morning service at St Dunawd's Church, which overlooked the River Dee. Ruth had passed the church the previous day and stopped at the war memorial that was to one side of its gate. She remembered reading the names of those men from the village who had died in the First World War. The plaque told of how the Ormrod family had lost three sons in three years. How did they ever recover from that? Did they believe that the sacrifice of those young men was justified? How had they felt when Britain entered another world war less than twenty years later?

Stubbing out her cigarette, Ruth sat up and stretched. The early promise of a sunny autumnal day had gone, as battleship grey clouds drifted west and filled the sky. They had drained the colour from the garden and the fields that swept away down the valley. It was time to go in.

She had just washed up her mug when someone knocked on the front door. As she opened it, Ruth saw the flawless, smiling face of her daughter Ella. Her big brown eyes sparkled.

'You're always early,' Ruth said, giving her a tight hug.

Ella stood back, ignoring her mother's comment. 'No offence, Mum, but you look like shit.'

They had that kind of relationship.

'Why does everyone think that saying the phrase "No offence" allows you to insult someone?' Ruth remarked, but knowing what her daughter had said was true.

'Are you sleeping?' Ella asked, taking Ruth's hand as they wandered into the kitchen.

'No,' Ruth admitted.

Gazing around, Ella pulled a face and dropped her mum's hand as she looked around the rather sparse room. 'I didn't realise that Sian had so much stuff. You need to get a few things to brighten up the house. A bunch of flowers would be a start.' The neglected clump of wilted foliage in a vase on the windowsill almost died on cue.

'I'm not sure life-affirming slogans and lots of cushions around the house are my thing,' Ruth said.

'I'll get you a few things,' Ella said, dumping out the contents of the vase into the bin.

Ruth turned and clicked the kettle on.

It had been a week since her partner Sian, a detective constable in the North Wales Police, had moved out, and Ruth wasn't dealing with it very well. They loved each other, but Ruth's preoccupation with the past had got in the way. After Ruth took an ill-advised trip to London in search of answers, Sian had finally had enough and decided to move on with her life. Without Ruth.

In fact, the trip to London had produced more questions than it had answered. Somewhere in the depths of London's underground railway network, Ruth had managed to lose the two men she suspected to be involved in Sarah's disappearance. The key to what had exactly happened to Sarah seven years ago seemed further away than ever. And now Ruth was on her own again.

The fact that both Ruth and Sian worked in Llancastell CID didn't help matters. It had been a frosty few days at work, and Ruth had spent most of it doing paperwork, hidden in the safety and comfort of her office.

As Ruth waited for the kettle to boil, she remembered all the fun and laughter that she'd had with Sian in that kitchen. Their little sayings and jokes. Cooking together with music blaring. It was all gone. The feeling of loss overwhelmed her as she blinked away a tear.

The kettle boiled and clicked noisily in the silence. The church bells of St Dunawd's sounded to signify the hour.

Ruth looked at Ella, pursed her lips together and wiped another tear that had fallen onto her cheek.

Ella walked over and gave her a hug. 'You're gonna be all right, Mum. You know that?'

'Am I?' Ruth said quietly.

'You always are,' Ella said. 'Do you want me to move back in for a while?'

If Ruth was being honest, she would have loved for her only daughter to move in. But Ella was making a life for herself. She had picked up the pieces of Ruth's chaotic life too often before, and at an impressionable age when it should have been Ruth looking after her daughter. Not the other way around.

'God, no. You'll nag me about my smoking, make me tidy every five seconds, and generally be a bit irritating,' Ruth said with a chortle.

'Oh, thanks very much,' Ella said, smiling back.

CHAPTER 3

ABU AND MEDHI WERE crouched behind a battered car in the car park of JW Jones Printers at the heart of Didsbury Industrial Estate. Abu's heart had slowed a little as he tried to catch his breath.

The tension was mounting. Glancing at his watch, it had been over ten minutes since Abu had put in the coded message that the flat had been raided. He and Medhi were now waiting to be picked up from the prearranged meeting place by other members of their group.

Abu checked his watch again. *Where are they?*

The police helicopter still thundered overhead. If they didn't arrive soon, it was only a matter of time before he and Medhi were found.

Pulling his dark red backpack up onto his shoulders, Mehdi blinked at Abu. *What was going on in Mehdi's mind?* He didn't look like a man who was confident that his martyrdom for the holy jihad, as laid out in the Koran, was going to bring about divine rewards. He looked terrified.

Abu moved closer and spoke in a virtual whisper. 'Remember, if we die today, it is in the way of Allah, brother. Remember, no one who enters the kingdom of paradise will need to return to this world again. We shall have the dark-eyed houris as our loving companions for ever. Cups of the purest wine brought to us by immortal youths for eternity.'

Mehdi nodded. He seemed lifted by Abu's words. *'Jazak Allah,'* Medhi said, bowing his head. *May Allah reward you.*

A growing noise interrupted their conversation. Shouts that got louder as police officers scoured the industrial estate. Getting closer and closer.

Would they get out of here? The tension in Abu's stomach tightened.

From somewhere, the sound of a vehicle.

About time, Abu thought. He craned his neck to look for their rescuers. They would be using a carpet delivery van as cover.

He couldn't see anything. The anxiety was making feel him sick.

The sound of the engine got louder and closer.

Definitely the sound of a van. This is it. We're getting out of here.

Abu shot Medhi a confident look of optimism.

'Ready to run?' Abu asked quietly.

Medhi nodded, raised himself up off his haunches and moved away from the cover of the car.

Abu already had their escape in his head. A ten-yard sprint, dive into the back of the van and safely away.

He looked up at Medhi, who was readying himself to run. But there was something on his face. It looked like a red dot of light. *Like something you might get from a child's toy*, Abu thought for a split second.

The dot got brighter, shaking around Medhi's face before settling in the middle of his forehead.

Shit!

'*Get your hands up where I can see them! Now!*' a voice thundered.

Abu froze, wondering if they had seen him.

And then more booming voices. '*Get your hands up and get down on your knees!*'

Medhi walked out from behind the car in a daze. The vehicle they had heard had been a Police Armed Response BMW X5.

Armed officers moved in with speedy precision.

Abu stood up and put his hands in the air. He knew if he made any sudden movements, they would shoot him dead. He wasn't prepared to die in a hail of bullets. That wasn't in the plan.

Dressed in full combat gear - Kevlar ballistic vests, field-style ballistic helmets and black balaclavas over their noses and mouths - the armed officers looked terrifying.

There was more aggressive shouting as the police moved swiftly and encircled Abu and Medhi in a matter of seconds.

'*Get down! Now! On your knees!*' an officer screamed, his Heckler & Koch MP5 submachine gun pointed at Abu's head.

The red light of the gun's laser sight moved momentarily onto his left eye. He squinted as he dropped to his knees, his hands held high. He felt every cell in his body freeze. Feeling sick, Abu's body began to shake uncontrollably.

'*Oi! Hands in the air or I* will *shoot you!*' the armed officer bellowed at Medhi.

Glancing up, Abu saw that Medhi was frowning as though he didn't quite understand what was going on. He was still standing and his hands were by his side.

For God's sake, Medhi, you're going to get yourself killed!

Turning around, Medhi looked at him.

'Get your hands up, now!'

Abu watched as Medhi put his hand towards the strap of his rucksack – maybe he was just going to take it off?

NO!

It didn't matter that the explosives weren't primed. The police didn't know that.

Crack! Crack! Crack!

Abu flinched at the deafening noise of the gun. The officer fired three rounds into Medhi's chest and head. His body crumpled like a lifeless doll onto the tarmac, just metres away from Abu. It had fallen so that his head was directly facing Abu. But what remained was not a face at all but a dark, black, bloody hole between the young man's eyebrows. His eyes were open, but unseeing and opaque.

Medhi was dead.

CHAPTER 4

IT WAS MID-AFTERNOON. Detective Sergeant Nick Evans of the North Wales Police looked over at his fiancée, Amanda. She was fast asleep in a large, padded armchair. Her chest rose and fell slowly with each breath as, subconsciously, her hand cradled her pregnant belly. What with the preparations for the baby, and ensuring that her father was as comfortable as possible after he'd taken a turn for the worse just over a week ago, she must have been exhausted. They had been at the Fairview Hospice on the outskirts of Llancastell since morning, visiting Amanda's father, Tony. Nick let her sleep on as he gazed at her resting face. With her ruddy cheeks and radiant skin, she was beautiful. He would do anything for her.

There were only a few days left until Amanda's due date, and Nick couldn't deny that the thought of becoming a father was making him very anxious; he was terrified of turning out like his own dad. However, in that moment, he was also struck by the magical thought of that unborn, beautiful, precious person growing inside Amanda. Part him, part Amanda. What would they become? He thought of the tiny hands. What would they do with their life? Despite some comments at work of 'Bet you'd like a son', Nick had no preference of gender. A healthy baby was all he wanted.

To his left, Tony stirred and groaned. His face was grey and drawn, his eye sockets dark and sunken. He was deteriorating

THE WHITE FOREST KILLINGS

fast. It was only a couple of weeks ago that Tony, Nick's dad Rhys, and him had been up watching and cheering at sports on the TV. And now ... What a vile, uncompromising disease cancer is. The whole experience had taken Nick back to the last time he had seen his mother in a hospice. He was only twelve years old. She had been diagnosed with ovarian cancer, and the disease had spread quickly and aggressively. As Nick left his mum at the hospice for the last time, she had promised that when she got better she would come home and cook Nick's favourite dinner – homemade sausage and onion pudding with gravy. He knew that she was just saying it, but that night he still prayed that she would get well. He promised God that he would do anything to see his mother recover. The next day she had died, and he and God were finished.

A large television screen was mounted on the far wall. The breaking BBC news of a police raid on a flat in Manchester was on a continual loop. They had shot one of the terrorists dead, and the other had been arrested. Nick was glad that in the provincial town of Llancastell the threat of terrorism was virtually zero. When he was at school, he'd had an Indian friend called Amit for a year or two before his family moved away. Amit had been bullied mercilessly – he was the only person in the school from an ethnic minority. Nick suspected that Amit might have been the only pupil from an ethnic minority in the school's history.

Tony's eyes opened. He looked up at Nick and smiled.

'You need to take her home, son,' Tony whispered, gesturing to Amanda.

'She's okay. Do you need anything?' Nick asked.

'A pint and a fag,' Tony joked. 'Maybe a lap dance.'

Nick smiled back. 'I'll see what I can do.'

Tony looked over at the television for a few seconds. 'Killed one of those bastards, didn't they?'

'Yeah,' Nick said.

'Shame they didn't just shoot the other bugger whilst they were at it,' Tony mumbled.

Nick didn't reply. He was a detective sergeant and wasn't sure how he felt about shooting terrorists in cold blood.

'I'm just glad I'm not in London or one of the big cities and having to deal with all that every day,' Nick said, but by the time he looked back at Tony he had fallen asleep again. The high doses of morphine were making him increasingly groggy.

In recent years Nick had spent several days completing the required Prevent training for all police officers in the UK. Prevent was a government-led programme where the police and various other agencies worked together to safeguard vulnerable people from being drawn into terrorism. It had been drafted as a response to the intel that showed how homegrown Islamic terrorists had become radicalised in the UK – to help avoid incidents like the one the news channel was showing. Nick couldn't get his head around it. Being in a parochial town in North Wales didn't help his understanding of the challenges faced by the multicultural, multifaith cities of Britain.

Checking his watch, Nick saw that it was nearly four o'clock. He would let Amanda sleep a little longer – she looked so peaceful and serene. It worried him that the stress of her father's illness was getting to her just when she needed to be calm. Since the early days of her pregnancy, she had been reiterating how desperately she wanted Tony to see the baby before he passed away. However, as the pregnancy went on, the more stressed Amanda became about the fact that Tony mightn't live to meet his grandchild.

Nick's phone buzzed. It was his boss in Llancastell CID, Detective Inspector Ruth Hunter.

'Boss?' Nick said, answering the phone and wandering away so as not to wake the others.

'You okay? Where are you?' Ruth asked.

'At the hospice with Amanda and Tony,' Nick replied.

'Right. Send them my best ... How's Tony?'

Nick looked over at Tony. 'No change. But he asked me for a pint, a fag and a lap dance, so he's still got his sense of humour.'

'I didn't know you performed lap dances,' Ruth quipped.

'Funny ... Weekend okay?'

Nick knew that Ruth had been struggling since her recent trip to London. He only knew a few details, but it hadn't turned out as she'd planned.

'Drake called me. He needs me and you in bright and early tomorrow,' Ruth said.

'How early is early?' Nick asked.

'Five thirty pick-up. That okay? You'll be up much earlier than that as soon as the little one comes,' Ruth said. She hadn't really needed to ask whether an early start was okay - but she was a superb team leader and a friend.

'Sure. Coffees are on him then ... What's going on?' Nick asked. It was unusual for DCI Ashley Drake to request such an early start.

'Not sure. He wouldn't say. He said officers from Special Branch were coming in to talk to us,' Ruth explained, sounding none the wiser.

'Special Branch? What are they doing in Llancastell?' Nick was taken aback. Special Branch usually dealt with national security and intelligence. Their job is essentially to protect the UK from threat and subversion. Within the force, the name Special Branch was mainly synonymous with terrorism.

'Drake was being annoyingly vague, so I don't know,' Ruth replied.

'No problem. I'll see you at five thirty then,' Nick said, wondering what all the cloak-and-dagger stuff was about.

CHAPTER 5

ABU STROLLED DOWN THE Vulnerable Prisoner wing at HMP Rhoswen. He'd been there a few years ago on remand for conspiracy, but the case never made it to trial. The VP wing was made up of sex offenders, grasses, bent police officers, and any other prisoners connected to the British justice system. They ate and exercised at different times to the rest of the prison population for their own safety.

Abu assumed he was being kept on the wing because of his notoriety. If word got out that he was the Islamic 'terrorist' – how he hated that word – who had been arrested the day before in Manchester, some far-right extremist or lunatic might try to kill him.

As he made his way towards his temporary single cell, most of the other prisoners were watching television, playing pool, or working out in the prison gym. He went up the green steel stairs and onto the landing of the first floor. The noise of his fellow prisoners' voices echoed around the empty ground floor.

There was a strip of light green painted right through the middle of the floor all the way along the wing. Everything else was various shades of grey – the doors, the walls, the ceilings.

Abu had been given a small neat cell, but they'd warned him that he might be moved on at any time. The cell was simple. A single bed with a blue blanket and green pillowcase. A television resting on a table, and beside it a stack of blue plastic bowls and a knife, fork and spoon.

Sitting down on his bed, Abu watched two men walk past and look in. One of them was an Asian man in his sixties. He looked like Abu's late father, Rohan.

For a moment, it took Abu back a decade to when everything in his life had changed. His father had a massive heart attack and died in his sleep. He was only fifty-three. His death rocked Abu to the core. His mother and close friends commented that it had seemed to change him.

It wasn't long before Abu began attending the university's Islamic society with his postgraduate friend, Imran, and together they successfully campaigned for a designated Muslim prayer room. Abu was openly critical of the university's rugby captain who had made anti-Islamic jokes. When the story of the captain's behaviour appeared in the local press – leaked by Abu, of course – the vice-chancellor had no option but to suspend the star sportsman. For Muslim students, it was a significant moral victory. Abu's reputation as a vociferous, militant presence on the university campus grew. When the Islamic society invited the radical preacher and cleric, Imam Omar Al-Hamedi, to give an inspirational speech in the university lecture hall, Abu and Imran knew they had found their calling. Their radicalisation was swift and profound. It wasn't long before they were running secret chatrooms, discussing the more controversial teachings of the Koran. Soon after, Imam Al-Hamedi himself had asked them to embark on holy jihad.

Abu's train of thought was broken as two men appeared at the cell door. From their suits and their general manner, he knew they were coppers. Special Branch, no doubt.

'Abu Habib?' the older man asked.

Abu nodded but didn't get up.

'Don't get too cosy, eh? Looks like you're going on a little trip to the countryside. Bit of fresh air will do you the world of good,' the younger one said with a smirk.

The older man nodded with a smile and added, 'Rumour has it that there are some spooks heading across the Atlantic to have a little chat with you. The CIA don't fuck about with people like you, Abu.'

Abu didn't like the sound of that one bit. 'That's all right. I prefer spooks to coppers. More brains, better personal hygiene, and decent suits,' he quipped.

Ruth pulled up outside Nick and Amanda's cottage in Dinas Padog. She looked at the car's orange digital clock – *5.25 am*. The sun wouldn't be rising for another two hours. The small Snowdonia village was dead to the world.

Tom Walker's recent album was playing on the car stereo. The irony of the song *'How Can You Sleep at Night?'* wasn't lost on Ruth as she sat and looked at the dreary morning sky. She would give anything to wake up after a decent night's sleep and feel fully rested.

Undoing the seatbelt, Ruth pulled down the sun visor and looked at herself in the mirror; she wasn't impressed by the woman who looked back at her.

Jesus! Admittedly the small yellow light did her no favours, but there was no denying that the past few days had aged her. Ruth looked at her red, bloodshot eyes and the heavy bags – more like suitcases – that sat under them. *I look ancient!*

Moving to Wales just over two and a half years ago was supposed to have been a wise decision - to relax and get away from the mounting stresses that had plagued her life while working for the Met in inner-city London. But it seemed no matter how far away she moved from her past, the ongoing mystery of her missing partner, Sarah, would follow. On 5 November 2013, Sarah Goddard had boarded a train from Crystal Palace to Victoria during the morning rush hour. But she never arrived. She had simply vanished off the face of the earth, and no one had seen or heard from her since. There had been no note, no explanation, nothing. Ruth had been understandably crushed. Her colleagues in the Met did everything they could to support and help her, but as weeks turned to months, and then years, Sarah's whereabouts still remained a total mystery.

Ever since then, Ruth had examined every shred of evidence, every fresh lead, in her quest to find out what had happened to the woman she had often described as 'the love of her life'. She had scrutinised every frame of CCTV from that day. Spoken to every witness. The emotional and psychological impact on Ruth had been overwhelming. There had been many sightings of Sarah around the globe – from New Zealand to Nevada. None of them ever amounted to anything. On several occasions, Ruth had found herself chasing after someone who had resembled Sarah. Each time, she had been crushed again when she realised her mistake.

When Ruth met Sian, once she started working at Llancastell, she felt she'd finally met someone with whom she could move forward. However, about two weeks ago, Ruth received information that Sarah had had an affair with a man named Jamie Parsons in the summer of 2013. Ruth felt compelled to dig deeper, convinced that Parsons had something to do with Sarah's disappearance. Having discovered that Ruth had secretly gone to London to meet Jamie Parsons, Sian said that enough was enough. She had already given Ruth an ultimatum – move on from Sarah's disappearance, or I'll leave. No matter how much Ruth wanted to, she couldn't let go of the new lead that might unveil the truth of what had happened in the winter of 2013. So Sian had packed her bags and left.

Opening the car door, Ruth could feel the cold bite of the wind on her face. It was just what she needed to wake her up. She ran her hands through her hair, and looped it behind her ears. It felt dry and coarse.

Pulling up the collar on her coat, she made her way down the stone steps and knocked on the door. A light flicked on inside. She remembered the first time she had picked Nick up from the cottage. It was a few months after she had arrived in North Wales, and he had stunk of booze. In fact, she was sure that Nick had had a drink before coming out of the front door. He had been a chronic but functioning alcoholic. However, Nick had turned his life around and had been sober for a couple of years. He regularly went to AA meetings and seemed transformed, and he was a much better copper for it. He told her frequently that it was a bloody miracle.

The locks on the door clicked, and the door opened.

'Oh, it's you,' Nick said with a sardonic grin.

'Come on, you plonker.' Ruth rolled her eyes.

'Plonker? Showing your age, aren't you?' Nick said, closing the door quietly behind him.

'I'm looking and feeling my age this morning too,' Ruth groaned.

'That bad is it?' Nick asked.

'Worse,' Ruth said as they walked down the path.

'Well, at least I woke up at the crack of dawn this morning. Nothing like it!' Nick said. She could see that he was trying to cheer her up.

Ruth shook her head. 'Is this going to be some terrible joke?'

'No. I like to wake up at the crack of dawn. She farts and then she makes me breakfast!' Nick quipped as they headed towards the car.

'Really? How old are you?' Ruth said.

'Physically, thirty-six. Mentally and emotionally, maybe twelve,' Nick laughed.

'Well, even though you're twelve, you're still driving,' Ruth said, tossing him the car keys.

They got in, and before Nick had started the engine Ruth's phone rang.

'Drake ...' Ruth mouthed to Nick as she answered it. 'Boss?'

'The boys from Special Branch are here already. I need to know if you and Nick's firearms training is up to date?' Drake asked.

Ruth felt her stomach flip. She hadn't held a gun for many years; her last firearms training had been during her Advanced Detective Course in London. The training authorised her to carry a handgun for five years. She knew that Nick had done advanced tactical firearms training in the last eighteen months. In fact, she had worried about just how much he had enjoyed it, and thought he might even leave Llancastell CID for a designated firearms unit.

'Yes, sir. We're both currently covered to carry firearms,' Ruth said, spotting Nick's confused expression.

What the hell was going on?

IT WAS GONE SIX THIRTY by the time Drake had ushered Ruth and Nick into the sizeable conference room on the fifth floor of Llancastell Police Station. CID was virtually empty except for a couple of young DCs on the night shift, and Drake had said nothing since they sat down. Ruth looked outside at the black sky that was only just starting to show signs of the pale light of dawn. She sipped her coffee and looked at Nick, who shrugged. She was getting a little fed up with all the covert bullshit.

Although the room was silent, they were not alone at the table. DI Gary Brunton, the male Special Branch officer, was middle-aged, balding, and stocky. He was wearing a tie that was way too thin and served only to exaggerate the width of his torso. Next to him sat DS Sally Perkins who Ruth guessed was in her thirties. She wore a serious look that seemed somehow forced. Ruth had an eye for people who weren't comfortable in their own skin and she was self-aware enough to know that, sometimes, that was her.

Taking off his jacket, Brunton took out a memory stick. As he hitched up his trousers, his stomach strained at his shirt buttons.

Surveillance work is not good for the waistline, Ruth thought - although given what she looked like this morning, she wasn't in a position to judge anyone's physical appearance.

Brunton wandered over to the computer. They had linked it up to a projector aimed at the wall.

'Sorry about the early start, guys. And apologies that you haven't been briefed as to why DS Perkins and I are here. We've only given DCI Drake the basic details.' Brunton dimmed the lights a little, inserted the memory stick into the computer, and clicked. A male South Asian face appeared on the wall.

'Okay. So, here's the brief overview of why we've come to talk to you this morning. The man you see here is Abu Habib, one of the terrorists that planned to detonate explosives in Manchester yesterday,' Brunton explained. 'Habib is thirty, and originally from Hemel Hempstead in Hertfordshire. He is the leader of various terrorist cells working out of Didsbury. They all have links to this man, the cleric Omar Al-Hamedi, who I am sure you are aware of.' Brunton clicked again, and another face appeared on the wall. 'Al-Hamedi has links to terror groups across the world and the Islamic State in Afghanistan. He is also responsible for the radicalisation of many of the homegrown terrorists we have identified in the North West.'

Nick shot Ruth a look as if to say, 'And this comes under our remit, how?' She was thinking exactly the same thing.

Brunton clicked again. 'Abu Habib was working with this man, Medhi Brahimi, a twenty-year-old activist from *Groupe Islamique Armé*, an extreme Algerian terror group. Counterterrorism officers shot and killed Brahimi yesterday. You probably will have seen it on the news,' he said.

'We think there were at least three other members of this terrorist cell in Manchester. Our intel tells us that they have explosives. We've got every available police officer in the Manchester Metropolitan area out there looking for them,' Perkins continued.

'Right, so this is where you guys come in.' Brunton clicked back to the photograph of Abu Habib. 'Special Branch and MI5 have Abu Habib in custody. We have transferred him from Manchester to HMP Rhoswen, which comes under the jurisdiction of North Wales Police. He's being held there on the VP wing.'

'Why not keep him in Manchester?' Nick asked.

'The prisons in Manchester are awash with Islamic extremists. It would be virtually impossible to stop Habib communicating with them. It's far safer for us to have him here in Wales,' Perkins explained.

Of course they had to choose Ruth's patch. This was the last thing she needed: babysitting terrorists.

'How does this involve us?' Ruth asked.

Brunton clicked again, and a picture of a large two-storey house built from stone and slate appeared on the wall. It was in the middle of a dense forest. 'This MI5 safe house is in the White Forest in the heart of Snowdonia National Park. No one knows it's there. Not even North Wales Police – until now, of course. Several CIA field agents are flying in to interrogate Habib in relation to the Miami bombings. They arrive on Wednesday. Habib is to stay at the safe house until then.'

Ruth didn't like the sound of this one bit. 'So you want us to take him there?'

Drake nodded. 'Yes. And this is coming from way over my head. The email I was forwarded last night had come via Whitehall.'

'What about officers from Manchester?' Ruth asked. She wasn't happy about CID officers being used to transfer a prisoner.

'Sorry. We're at breaking point already looking for the rest of Habib's terrorist group,' Brunton explained.

'MI5?' Ruth asked, already knowing the answer.

'MI5 agents will meet you at the safe house this afternoon. They will take over once they arrive,' Drake explained. 'Sorry, Ruth. I want experienced officers on this.'

'Bloody hell,' Ruth said.

Drake shook his head. 'I know this is bullshit, but my hands are tied.'

Ruth couldn't hide her annoyance, and suspected there was more bullshit to come.

'How long?' Nick asked, sounding anxious.

'Twenty-four hours at the most. And it's okay, Nick, you drive Habib up there with Ruth. MI5 take over from you late afternoon and you can go.' Drake looked at the Special Branch officers. 'Nick is about to become a father any day now.'

'Congratulations,' Perkins said.

'Thanks,' Nick said, but Ruth could see he wasn't happy either. They both could have done with a day sitting doing paperwork and drinking coffee.

Ruth wasn't hiding her annoyance very well. It was the kind of crap that angered her about the Met. Special Branch, or some other division of national security, would swan in and expect hardworking police officers to drop everything they were doing to do their dirty work.

'Don't worry, Ruth. Habib will be handcuffed to a uniformed officer for the entire journey. No one knows that Habib is in Wales. And no one knows where the safe house is. It's just a bit of babysitting until MI5 get here. Take a book,' Drake said.

'Then why are we taking firearms?' Ruth snapped.

'Just a precaution. It'll make you feel safer. And it's just a suggestion,' Drake said.

Ruth nodded. It wasn't that she felt she was in danger, it was just a pain in the arse being stuck in the middle of Snowdonia for twenty-four hours twiddling her thumbs when she had a mountain of paperwork to catch up on.

CHAPTER 6

12.08 pm

ABU SAT NEAR TO THE processing area of HMP Rhoswen. They had given him little information except that he was being transferred. He leant forward and stretched out his legs in an effort to loosen his hamstrings. They felt a little tight after sleeping all night curled up on the narrow prison bed that was a bit too short for him.

His hands were cuffed, and he rested them on his lap as he gazed around. The metal felt heavy and cold on his skin. A female prison officer, who sat behind a protective screen, gave him a filthy look. He was used to it. In fact, it gave him a feeling of strength. He knew she was judging him. Abu didn't understand how Western society could allow women such freedom and independence. The purdah beliefs that he had about the seclusion of women came from his feeling that the chastity and dignity of women was sacrosanct. Women were vulnerable and needed to be protected. Abu was angry that these views were so bitterly criticised in a society where prostitution, sex trafficking, pornography, rape, and paedophilia were endemic. Look at the effect of the West's liberal attitudes. Women had less respect, worth, and protection than they ever had. How could their society let them down like that? It disgusted him.

Abu watched a young man in his early twenties being processed. His head was shaved and his arms covered in tattoos. He was the stereotype of every white prisoner Abu had ever met.

A radio was on somewhere, and the cricket commentary from the BBC's Test Match Special burbled. Cricket had always been Abu's sport. As a left-arm spin bowler, he had been picked for the district cricket team and then for Hertfordshire County. He idolised the Pakistani cricket player Abdul Qadir Khan, who had been the best spin bowler in the world during the seventies and eighties. For a while, there had been talk of Abu playing cricket professionally, until he damaged the tendons in his shoulder.

Three police officers, only one in uniform, arrived at the central booking desk. A prison officer pointed to Abu – they were here to pick him up. He pretended not to see them. He didn't want to give them any inkling that he cared who they were or why they were there. They were nothing to him. Instruments of an infidel state that claimed to promote democracy and freedom, but blatantly abused the human rights of its citizens for its own ends.

'Abu Habib?' the female officer asked. She had a London accent.

Abu looked up, said nothing, and just stared at her. By her manner and confidence, she must be the boss. Internally, Abu fumed. It wasn't what Allah had intended. Women were meant to be grandmothers, mothers, sisters, aunts and daughters. They were *not* meant to be police officers!

'Like that, is it?' the female officer said, raising an eyebrow. 'We're taking you to a location in North Wales today, Mr Habib. May I call you Abu?' When he didn't answer, she carried on. 'The journey is around forty minutes and you will be handcuffed to PC Garrow' – she indicated the young uniformed officer – 'for the duration of that journey. Once we have you in the secure location, the handcuffs can come off.'

Abu noticed that the female officer had a calm surety that was often lacking in her male counterparts, who seemed to feel a constant need to show their strength and superiority.

'Where are we going?' Abu asked.

'Mini-break,' the male plainclothes officer joked.

Abu took an immediate dislike to him. He seemed to be overcompensating for something.

Whilst she unlocked the cuff from his left wrist, Abu noticed a scar on the female officer's left hand. Abu looked down at his own left hand. He had a deep scar across all five knuckles. He had got it while defending himself from a gang of kids in Watford whose idea of a good night out was a spot of drunken 'Paki-bashing'. It had left him hospitalised for three days.

The female detective smelled of cigarettes laced with faint traces of perfume, which Abu thought made her seem cheap and sleazy. It was how most Western women smelled.

Abu was then handcuffed to PC Garrow. He was young, and clearly nervous about being attached to a terrorist for the next hour or so. Abu was glad. He wanted the young man to be afraid. Fear was a powerful tool in the Islamic jihad.

'Don't worry, he doesn't bite,' the male plainclothes officer said to Abu as he gestured to PC Garrow. 'Well, if he does, it's only playful.'

Abu ignored the man's childish jokes. Grabbing his small bag of possessions with his free hand, he and the three police officers went through a series of security gates before entering the car park.

The air was cold and crisp. Abu slowed and took a deep breath, but PC Garrow was in a hurry to get to the car.

Abu allowed himself a small smile. If PC Garrow knew what was going to happen later, he might not have been in such a hurry.

12.37 pm

RUTH AND NICK HAD BEEN to the North Wales Police Armoury and signed out two handguns, plus the ammunition to go with them. Most UK police forces favoured the Glock 17 9mm pistol. Nick, as the resident gun bore, had explained that the Glock utilised the double-stack magazine, which held seventeen rounds of 9x9mm Parabellum ammunition. Neither Ruth nor Nick were happy about carrying a handgun, but sometimes it was part of the job.

They had picked Abu Habib up from HMP Rhoswen with relative ease, and now he was sitting silently in the back of the Astra, handcuffed to PC James Garrow, tall, lean, and wearing thin-framed glasses – the poor sod from Uniform who'd been assigned to join them.

Sitting in the passenger seat, Ruth gazed out at the countryside. They passed through the small town of Bethesda, named after its famous chapel. As they cut south on the A470, Ruth saw the adverts for Zip World near Blaenau Ffestiniog. It was an outdoor activity park set in the Penrhyn Quarry, once the world's largest slate quarry. She, Sian and Ella had visited there back in August and travelled on the Deep Mine Tour that took them five hundred feet down into the disused slate caverns. Sian suffered from claustrophobia and held Ruth's hand throughout, closing her eyes when things got too much. Ruth had refused to join her daughter on Velocity 2, the world's fastest zip wire that took you over the quarry lake. Instead, she and Sian had drunk coffee in the observation cafe and watched Ella fly overhead at over one hundred miles an hour. It had been a fantastic day. A perfect day.

Sitting up and stretching out her shoulders, Ruth couldn't help but think of Sian. What a monumental disaster she had made of their relationship. Ruth desperately wanted to believe that there was a way back for them but, deep down, she knew that Sian would never trust her again. A few days ago, DCI Drake had come to tell her that Sian had put in a transfer request for a detective constable job down in Cardiff. It had broken Ruth's heart. They really were over. Even though it was never spoken about openly, Ruth knew that most officers in CID knew of her and Sian's relationship. She assumed that's why Drake had asked her if she was okay when discussing Sian's transfer request.

Putting herself in Sian's shoes, Ruth knew that she had given Sian no choice but to leave. She would have done the same thing in Sian's position. But what was she supposed to do? Stop looking for Sarah altogether? Accept that she was dead? Give up hope of finding out what had happened to her on that fateful morning?

Ruth looked over at Nick, who was deep in thought. If she didn't occupy her mind soon, she would be engulfed in grief and self-pity.

'All okay, sarge?' Ruth asked.

'Marvellous, boss,' Nick said with a sardonic smile, and gestured to the satnav. 'ETA, twenty minutes.'

'Looking forward to paternity leave?' Ruth asked. Glancing into the wing mirror, she noticed a black van behind them. It pulled out for a few seconds as it tried to overtake them.

Bloody idiots. It's a single-lane road.

'Of course. No sleep, nappies, shit. What's not to like?' Nick said.

'Living the dream, eh?' Ruth said.

Nick frowned as he looked in the rear-view mirror.

'Problem?' Ruth asked.

'I don't know. That van has been behind us since we passed the turning to Ruthin,' Nick said quietly.

'Yeah, I just noticed it trying to overtake us.' Ruth leant down to look in the wing mirror again. She could now see it was a black Renault. At this range, she couldn't see the driver or if anyone else was in the van.

'What do you think?' Ruth said.

Nick took his right hand from the steering wheel. He placed it onto the gear stick.

'I think we'll see how determined this van is to stick with us,' Nick said. He dropped the car from fifth to fourth gear.

Ruth felt the two-litre engine kick in, and the acceleration pushed her back in her seat. Abu was getting restless in the back. Maybe he thought there was a chance of a rescue. Her pulse started to increase. She looked down at the small locked armoury compartment by her feet and regretted attaching its key to her car keyring. In any case, she did not want to be using a handgun today.

Suddenly, Nick pulled the Astra out onto the other side of the road. They overtook a sluggish caravan. Glancing over, she saw that they were doing eighty miles an hour. They had gone past the caravan in a flash, as though it was stationary.

Ruth spun around anxiously. She saw that the black van had overtaken the caravan too. That wasn't surprising, given the slow speed of the caravan, but it worried her a little. Her palms were feeling a little sweaty.

Are we actually being chased?

'Can you see the plate?' Ruth asked Nick.

'Not really,' Nick said.

Ruth clicked the Tetra radio. 'Control from three-six. We have a suspect vehicle tailing us. Southbound on the A-four-seven-zero. I'm going to need a PNC check.'

'Three-six, received. Standing by,' the CAD (Computer Aided Dispatch) operator said.

Nick was staring in the rear-view mirror. 'Sorry, boss. Still can't see it. And I've got good vision.'

Ruth glanced behind. Abu looked directly at her with a smirk.

'Is there a problem, detective?' Abu asked, raising his eyebrows.

Don't be a smug wanker.

Ruth ignored him but she could see that PC Garrow was looking worried.

'Right, fuckwit – let's see how fast you want to go,' Nick said as he took the car up to ninety. Then to a hundred.

They hit a bend. Ruth felt herself being pushed hard towards the passenger door. She gripped the seat and squinted.

They flew past a road sign. The car edged over a hundred miles an hour.

Ruth glanced in the wing mirror. The black van was only about three hundred yards behind.

Fuck! This is not good. She glanced again at the gun compartment.

They hurtled around a long bend. Ruth felt the Astra's back tyres skid. They were going too fast.

'Change of tack,' Nick said. They hit a long straight stretch of road.

Touching the brakes, Nick reduced the speed. Ninety miles an hour, eighty, seventy.

Ruth spun around. What would the van do now? Slow down to follow? Try to stop their car? Drive on?

The black van pulled out to overtake. Ruth held her breath. Her pulse was racing.

It drew level with them. The black side panels looked ominous.

What if they slide open to reveal a gunman? Don't be ridiculous, Ruth! We're in Snowdonia, not Compton!

Ruth looked over. She saw a woman in a red bandana and round sunglasses who smiled and gave the peace sign.

The van accelerated away into the distance. Ruth could see that there were two mountain bikes secured to the back.

Adrenaline junkie hippies. She knew the type.

'Looks like they're just out for a cycling day,' Ruth muttered as her pulse slowed.

The van eventually disappeared out of sight.

'Yeah, looks like a false alarm, boss,' Nick said, puffing his cheeks out.

Ruth nodded, but this wasn't the gentle drive into Snowdonia that she had imagined.

1.26 pm

TWENTY MINUTES LATER, Nick drove up to the tall
black gates that led to the safe house. They had travelled at least
five miles off the main road, and they were deep into the shadowy forest.

The rest of the journey had remained uneventful. It reminded Ruth of the time she had brought the notorious serial
killer, Andrew Gates, to Snowdonia to identify the places
where he had buried his victims. Snowdonia had been dusted
with snow that day and it had been bitterly cold. Ruth remembered that the operation had also been an abject failure. The
repercussions of it had been deadly.

Getting out of the car, Ruth noticed that the air outside
was strangely humid for the time of year, and smelled of the
dampness and mulch of rotting autumnal leaves. The forest itself dated back ten thousand years to the last ice age. With its
range of enormous Atlantic oak trees, Ruth had seen that under the darkening canopy, the ground was criss-crossed with
streams and gullies. Standing alongside the gnarled, ancient
oak trees were also tall trunks of ash, hazel and birch. Under-
foot, she trod on lichens, moss and liverworts.

The wind sighed through the trees. It was an eerie, almost
sorrowful sound that made Ruth shiver. She turned and gazed
into the impenetrable darkness of the surrounding forest. Anyone or anything could be out there. Hiding in the shadows,

scenting them on the breeze. The speedy onset of winter darkness was making her feel very uneasy.

Suddenly there was movement as something emerged from the canopy and flew overhead, flicking branches and leaves noisily. Ruth flinched and dropped into a crouch. Nick wound down the window and laughed at his senior officer. 'You all right, boss? It's only bats. The forest is home to the black horseshoe bat – harmless! More scared of you than you of it.'

Ruth wasn't going to hang around to find out. The thought of the dark furry creatures flying above her made her shudder. As far as she was concerned, bats were the gothic creatures from horror films. After all, there weren't many bats native to South London.

Pretending that she hadn't been spooked, and taking out her phone, Ruth read the code she'd been given for the electronic gates. She wandered over to them - looking above her for any more winged creatures that might want to swoop down at her - and noticed that the enormous wrought iron gates were cemented into two towering stone pillars. Even though the gates were relatively new, vivid-green moss and dark ivy cascaded in waves to the ground and covered the stone of the pillars and the surrounding ten-foot walls.

Ruth punched the five-digit number into the electronic pad. *6-5-2-2-9.* There was a mechanical click and the gates swung open slowly. At that moment the wind moaned again, this time louder. The powerful gust scattered leaves around her feet, as though their arrival had been noted by the surrounding woods. *Bloody hell, this place is creepy.*

Following the car up the long gravel driveway, the safe house loomed into view. The renovated building was a large two-storey house made from local stone. It gave Ruth a curious shrinking feeling, as though her life force had faded while the house and the surrounding forest had doubled in size. It towered above her like a sinister presence, dwarfing them all with an unnerving, timeless power.

The car pulled to a halt in front of the main entrance and Ruth opened the back door of the car to let PC Garrow get out with Abu still attached by handcuffs. The gates closed behind them with a clunk. A spell of silence stained the air for a few seconds.

'Everything okay, constable?' Ruth asked, breaking the uneasy quiet.

'Yes, ma'am. No problem,' Garrow replied.

Abu frowned. 'Can you take these things off me? I'm not going anywhere.'

'When we get inside,' Ruth said as she looked for the coded drop box that housed the keys. She had a code for that too.

'Just imagine what you would have paid on Airbnb for a place like this,' Nick said to Abu.

PC Garrow chortled a little too hard – Ruth could see he was trying to make a good impression with them. She had been the same as a young PC.

Ruth went to the lockbox and retrieved the keys, the security alarm code, and a floor plan of the house.

She tried the largest key first, turned it in the lock, and door opened with ease.

In front of them was a large hallway that looked more like that of a hotel or office suite than of a secret safe house. It smelled of new carpets, but also had the mustiness of a house that had been originally built in the mid-1800s. Central to the hallway was a large, wide staircase that split both ways as it reached the first floor. The house was far lighter and airier than Ruth had imagined it would be.

Even though the operation had gone smoothly so far – bar the scare with the van – Ruth had a nagging sense of unease as the group went inside. There was nothing to worry about, so she assumed it was because she was out of her comfort zone – or perhaps because inside the safe house was a little chilly. Ruth was, if anything, a creature of habit and routine.

'Constable, there is a holding cell on the first floor. I have the code so I will take you and the prisoner upstairs in a minute,' Ruth explained.

However, now that they were inside, Ruth noticed the high-pitched continuous beeping of what must have been an electronic alarm. She glanced around, looking for its source.

'What's that?' Nick asked with a frown.

'It must be the alarm.' Ruth scanned the walls for a number pad. There was a square grey box with a digital readout.

Ah-ha! She went over, glanced at the four-digit number on the laminated piece of card and entered the code. She pressed 'Enter' and waited for the alarm to stop beeping.

Nothing.

It continued to beep and flash red.

Ruth entered the code again.

Still nothing.

'That's going to be annoying,' Abu said, with a smile like he had just bitten into a lemon.

'Shut up,' PC Garrow muttered.

Ruth peered at the readout: *System Restart – No Connection Found.*

Nick came over and glanced at the display. They shared a look.

Does that mean that the alarm system isn't working? Or has the alarm been set off? Ruth wondered. She wasn't going to say it in front of Abu.

'Stay there. I'll be back in a second,' Ruth said. She headed left for what she could see from the floor map was the kitchen.

Moving slowly through the ground floor of the house, Ruth found the stillness and quiet eerie. The empty walls added to the feeling of starkness. The distant noise of the alarm made her jittery. Then another noise that came from somewhere – a strange gurgle. Then a judder of something metallic.

Ruth froze and listened. *What the bloody hell was that?*

Not daring to move, she wondered whether someone coming into the house had tripped the alarm before they arrived. *What if someone else was already here?*

The noise then stopped abruptly. Maybe it had been the central heating or water pipe?

The door to the downstairs toilet further down the corridor was wide open.

A couple of amber leaves crunched under her foot. She glanced down at them.

How long have they been there? More importantly, where did they come from?

Then she came to the kitchen. It was functional, but new-looking. Cupboards and surfaces were cream. Ruth shivered – the temperature dropped further with every step deeper into the building.

The hum of the fridge seemed to be loud and urgent in the stillness. It rattled.

Ruth's eyes were drawn to the cooker where a time display flashed rhythmically with *00.00.*

Phew! Ruth gave a sigh of relief. She knew what that meant. The electricity had gone off at some point and everything had reset itself. That's why the alarm was sounding. It's happened in her place at least every couple of months, and momentary power failures were common in North Wales.

Wandering back to the hallway, Ruth looked at Nick. 'It's all right. Just a power cut that's reset everything.'

Tapping on the buttons of the alarm box, Ruth pressed reset and the noise stopped.

What a relief! There was something about the place that was making her jumpy, and she mustn't let it get to her.

'Right, let's get sir upstairs and settled,' Ruth said to PC Garrow, gesturing to Abu.

'Boss, I'll have a check around outside,' Nick said, going to the front door.

Ruth led the way up the wooden steps and onto the landing where the functional grey carpet was hardly worn.

Following behind with PC Garrow, Abu Habib had a calm assuredness to his manner. It was uncharacteristic of most prisoners that she'd encountered. His face remained set in a look of calm serenity, as if he were casually checking out a house on the market as opposed to being introduced to the place where he was to be held captive. Then again, Abu Habib wasn't the usual profile of criminals in Llancastell.

'I think it's down here,' Ruth said, looking at the floor plans.

Glancing at Abu's face, he had the look of someone who was confident they knew more than everyone else. It wasn't quite a smirk, but Ruth found it unsettling.

At the end of the corridor, there was a steel door with another electronic code pad on the wall beside it. Ruth put in yet another code, marvelling that in her tired state she hadn't got them mixed up. She opened the door and gestured for Abu and PC Garrow to go inside the holding cell.

Ruth glanced around the room. It looked like the kind of room you would find in a bland business hotel chain. She knew that the rooms in the house weren't always used for criminals. Often, they were used for people who were vulnerable witnesses, or even those who had gone into Witness Protection. When she was in the Met, there had been a variety of innocuous-looking safe houses at their disposal. Sometimes witnesses and their families had to stay in them for months while they waited to give evidence at trial. It wasn't much of a life. Ruth often wasn't surprised when witnesses decided they'd rather keep quiet and were no longer willing to testify – especially in cases against organised criminals. Months, or even years, in these places was enough to test the hardiest of souls.

Ruth checked that the window was securely locked. She could see that it was made from reinforced glass. Abu wasn't going anywhere, but she wasn't taking any chances.

'Okay, constable, you can take the cuffs off,' Ruth said. 'But I want him cuffed to the bed to be on the safe side.'

Abu raised his eyebrows. 'Curious that you fear me even in a locked room.'

Ruth ignored him. He was trying to get a rise out of her.

PC Garrow unlocked the handcuffs and Abu rubbed his wrists. He then led Abu to the bed and cuffed his hand to the left-hand side of the bedframe.

Ruth looked at Abu, whose face was expressionless. 'You'll be in here from now on. I'll come back in a while when you can have a bathroom break. I'll see if I can get you some water.'

Abu deliberately ignored her.

Fuck him, if he's going to be rude, Ruth thought.

Giving PC Garrow a nod, they went out, and she closed the steel door behind her.

'Right. I'll get my bag in and then let's see if we can sort out a cup of tea, eh?' Ruth said with a smile of relief.

She had got the prisoner to the safe house, and he was secure in the holding cell. Now it was just a matter of waiting for the MI5 agents to arrive, and then she could relax.

CHAPTER 7

3.12 pm

HAVING BROUGHT IN HER bag and found a small bedroom on the first floor, Ruth wandered downstairs and headed for the kitchen. She found PC Garrow beside the kettle with three mugs, teabags, sugar, and long-life milk.

'Thank God for that,' Ruth said at the thought of a cup of tea. 'It's James, isn't it?'

'Yes, ma'am. But most people call me Jim,' he explained as the water boiled and the kettle clicked off.

'How long have you been on the job, Jim?' Ruth asked. Now that she could see him in the bright lights of the kitchen, she saw how young he was. No more than early twenties.

'Eighteen months, ma'am,' he replied as he busied himself making the tea.

'So, you're still a probationer then?' Ruth got a flashback to when she was a probationer in Battersea, South London, in the nineties. It felt like such a long time ago. Like a different lifetime.

'Six months to go, if everything goes well, ma'am,' PC Garrow said.

'Bright lad, then? Where did you get your degree?' Recruits who came into the North Wales Police with a degree were on probation for two years. If they came in the apprenticeship route, it was three years.

'Bangor. Criminology and Criminal Justice.' PC Garrow poured milk into the mugs.

Ruth raised her eyebrows. 'Wow. Impressive stuff. I got a couple of O levels and that was it. Do you want to stay in uniform?'

'No, ma'am. I want to work in CID. I always have done,' he answered.

'I'll bear that in mind if anything comes up,' Ruth said. She liked PC Garrow's quiet confidence. CID could always do with another bright and enthusiastic DC.

He smiled and nodded. 'Thank you, ma'am ... How long have you been in the force - if you don't mind me asking?'

'I don't mind at all. Coming up to thirty years. Twenty-five years in the Met. Then I came up here nearly three years ago,' Ruth explained.

Christ, he must think I'm a dinosaur, Ruth thought.

But if he did think that he didn't show any sign, and continued to stir the tea before turning to her with an open smile. 'Why did you move up here?' the young constable asked. He must have been genuinely interested, and Ruth was glad that he was starting to relax a little and not calling her *ma'am* every five seconds.

'That's a long story ... I thought it would be a quieter pace of life. But boy did I get that wrong,' Ruth said, thinking back on all the cases she had been an SIO on since arriving in Llancastell.

'It's never boring, is it? This job?' PC Garrow said, and then gestured to the mugs. 'Sugar for anyone?'

Ruth pulled a face. 'Not for me. But I think DS Evans usually has his bodyweight in sugar in his tea.'

PC Garrow frowned. 'Sorry, ma'am?'

'It's all right, Jim. I'm joking. Two spoons should do him. Get yourself settled. There's some kind of lounge with a telly in there. A few books. It's going to be fairly boring, sitting around until MI5 decide to grace us with their presence. And then some more sitting around,' Ruth explained.

'Yes, thank you, ma'am. Let me know if you need anything else,' PC Garrow said.

Ruth grabbed the two mugs of tea and wandered out into the hallway. 'DS Evans?' she yelled. The noise resounded up the stairwell and echoed slightly.

Nothing. Nick had been heading outside to have a look around and to check everything was all right while Ruth and PC Garrow were taking Abu Habib to his cell. He must have still been outside.

'DS Evans?' Ruth called again as she went over to the front door that was still slightly ajar. She felt the tepid autumnal wind blow through the gap, and could smell the scent of the trees and leaves outside. As she sipped her tea, she closed the door against the restless whine of the wind.

Now there was silence.

Where is he? The house isn't that big.

She listened for any kind of response. Nothing except the odd creak and groan from within the house as the wind intensified outside and sniffed its way in through the gaps in windows and eaves.

'Nick?' Ruth thundered. She felt uneasy.

'In here, boss. You need to check this out,' Nick shouted from a room across the hallway.

'Bloody hell. I was calling for you,' Ruth said, as she came into a compact room full of monitors, computers and wires.

Nick was sitting in a large office chair behind a bank of screens and a computer keyboard. 'This place is like a bloody fortress.'

'It's an MI5 safe house, Nick. What did you expect? It's not Scout camp,' Ruth said sarcastically, as she put his mug of tea down beside him and sat on a nearby chair.

'Yeah, but you wanna see some of this stuff. Motion sensors, cameras in every room and outside. Thermal imaging at night. We can control every light in this place and the garden from here,' Nick said, as he clicked the buttons and looked at the monitors.

'I know that Amanda finds the little nerdy boy routine charming, Nick. But sometimes it's boring,' Ruth said with a grin.

'You didn't understand half the stuff I said, did you?' Nick asked with a wry smile.

'Nope. Nor do I want to. I still refer to "taping television programmes" at home,' Ruth admitted.

'Luddite,' Nick said as he sipped his tea. 'Two sugars, nice one.'

'News on Evans Junior yet?' Ruth asked.

Nick sat back in the chair, sipped his tea and shook his head. 'No, nothing. Not the faintest hint of an appearance.'

'September birth. What star sign will that make them?' Ruth asked.

Nick rolled his eyes. 'Star sign? Really?'

'It's Virgo, isn't it? Yeah. My old man was a Virgo,' Ruth said, nodding.

'And what was he like?' Nick asked.

'Dishonest, unreliable, loving, generous, reckless,' Ruth said, thinking back to her chaotic upbringing in Battersea, most of which had been due to her father's unpredictable behaviour.

'And that's Virgo, is it?' Nick said with a frown.

'No, you pillock. That's what my old man was like. Virgos are reserved, sensitive, and artistic, aren't they?' Ruth said, finishing her tea – she might pop outside for a ciggie.

'What happened to your dad then?' Nick asked.

'God knows. He probably lied about his date of birth. He lied about everything else,' Ruth said.

She remembered her dad picking up her and her brother, Chris, and swinging them around somewhere in Battersea Park. Perhaps the negativity she had carried around towards her father when she was younger was misplaced. Maybe she had been looking for someone to blame for her own shortcomings? The dishonesty and recklessness she had shown in past relationships. He'd had his faults, but her dad had never been malicious or violent, and he had done what he thought was his best. When she examined her own track record as a parent, Ruth knew she wasn't in a position to judge anyone.

'Bit of a minefield though, isn't it?' Nick said.

'Fatherhood?' Ruth said. She knew how worried Nick was about becoming a father.

'You're nothing like your dad. You do know that? What's more, because of what you went through, you'll do everything in your power to be the best dad you can be,' Ruth said.

Nick gave her a slightly awkward smile. He never could take any compliments or praise.

'Anything from Drake?' Nick asked.

'Not yet,' Ruth said.

Ruth felt a buzz on her phone and saw that Steven Flaherty had sent her an email. She walked back to a low sofa behind the desk of screens, knowing that whatever news was in the email, she'd want to be sitting down.

Steven was the Met's liaison officer for the Missing Persons Unit. Since 2013, he had worked on Sarah's disappearance; he looked into viable leads and any new information. Ruth had nothing but admiration for him, and he had been incredibly supportive and kind over the years.

Ruth opened the message.

Hi Ruth,

Hope this email finds you well? Still struggling to establish more links between Jamie Parsons and Jurgen Kessler. However, I agree that the evidence is mounting up. It might be something I can take upstairs to see if they can free up some more manpower, considering the fresh evidence about Sarah's disappearance.

I will outline what we know to date. Jamie Parsons and Jurgen Kessler studied at the Berlin School of Economics at the same time, before working at the same bank in London. Jamie Parsons introduced Sarah to Jurgen Kessler at an elite sex party in London. Jamie Parsons had an affair with Sarah in the summer before she went missing, and they continued to attend these elite sex parties. From the CCTV footage that we have, we strongly believe that Jurgen Kessler was the last person to talk to Sarah on the morning of her disappearance. Kessler is now wanted in connection with the murder of two young women in Berlin. He entered the UK last year on a false passport and tried to gain employment at several universities. Last weekend, you met Jamie Parsons in

London. You followed him to Great Portland Street tube station, where you saw him meet Jurgen Kessler. You continued to follow them onto the London Underground but then lost them.

I have also attached a recent article from a tabloid newspaper about the Secret Garden parties.

If there is anything else you would like to add to this, please let me know in the next few days.

Yours, Steven

Ruth took a moment to digest what Steven had outlined in his email. It was a little overwhelming to see it all there, written in a clear paragraph. When she read it in such a succinct form, the evidence that Jurgen Kessler and Jamie Parsons were somehow involved in Sarah's disappearance seemed overwhelming, but there was no proof. What Ruth wanted was for the Met Police to re-open the case and pull Jamie Parsons in for questioning. She had seen him with a man who was wanted by the Berlin police and Interpol in connection with two murders. Surely that would be enough to call him in? How would he explain that?

'That's weird,' Nick said, breaking Ruth's train of thought. She looked over and saw him peering intently at the bank of monitors.

'What's up?' Ruth asked. She put her phone away and joined Nick at the desk again.

'All the cameras seem to work except that one, which is marked "Garden Camera – Garage Door",' Nick explained.

'Not a surprise, one camera out of about seventy not working, is it?' Ruth asked.

Nick shrugged. 'I don't know. I suppose not.'

'Do you want to have a look?' Ruth asked. She wasn't particularly worried, but she wanted to go outside for a ciggie before taking water up to Abu.

'Not much else to do. And you haven't had a fag for nearly two hours,' Nick said with a smile.

'You know me so well, Nicholas,' Ruth said, arching an eyebrow.

They went out into the hall and opened the heavy front security door. The sun was falling behind the trees, casting a crimson glow on the clouds and mountains in the distance. It would soon be dark and there had been no word from Drake about when the MI5 agents were due to arrive. All they had been told was 'late afternoon'. Ruth thought about the mounting paperwork sitting back on her desk at Llancastell nick and didn't mind putting it off for a little longer, but she wanted Nick to be back in town as soon as possible to be with Amanda. That was far more important than all this Special Branch and MI5 bullshit. It was just like the guys from London to expect the 'yokel' police to do their dirty work for them. Abu Habib wasn't their problem, and she was angry on Nick's behalf.

Nick stopped on the porch step and looked west, over to where the sun was setting.

'You see that peak?' Nick said, pointing.

Ruth peered and saw the dark plum shape in the distance, rising from behind the forest. 'What am I looking at?'

'Moel Siabod,' Nick replied.

'Same to you,' Ruth said with a smile. Ever since they had first met, Nick had been recounting proudly to Ruth these little nuggets of local Welsh history and folklore. She was outwardly facetious about it, rolling her eyes or teasing him, but in reality she thought it was endearing that he had such pride in the area he came from. It reminded her of her grandfather, Bill Hunter. He had been a proud cockney and loved to tell her tales of South London. He claimed that in the late 1930s a polar bear had escaped from London Zoo, and he had watched it swim in the Thames from Battersea Bridge. He also told her that Hitler had identified Du Cane Court, an art deco block of flats in Balham, as his intended residence in London when he successfully invaded Britain. Apparently, it had been secretly built so that it looked like a swastika from the sky. She was never sure whether to believe him, but that wasn't the point. It was his joy and pride at telling her stories that had been so magical.

'It's a mountain. *Moel Siabod* is Welsh for "shapely hill",' Nick explained.

Ruth arched her eyebrow. 'Always knew you had an eye for a shapely hill.'

Nick rolled his eyes. 'Do you want me to stop?'

'No, no. Sorry, go on,' Ruth said. She smiled to show that she meant it.

'The mountain lies between Betws-y-Coed and Capel Curig,' Nick said.

'Even I know where they are,' Ruth said proudly.

'Another older translation of the word *siabod* is "bare hill, a crown that is covered in newly fallen snow",' Nick explained.

'Well, I definitely prefer that translation,' Ruth admitted, thinking what a lovely image that was.

'And beyond that, can you see the mist on those high ridges on the horizon?' Nick asked.

'Yes,' said Ruth as she squinted. A thin band of what almost looked like smoke drifted slowly along the undulating edge of the mountainous horizon. It was stunning.

'That's the tops of Twll Du, which is this incredible valley known as the Devil's Kitchen. The valley was formed when the rock split two thousand years ago,' Nick explained.

'That seems pretty recent, if I remember my geography,' Ruth said, hoping she didn't sound stupid.

'Yes, it is. The last ice age finished over ten thousand years ago,' Nick explained. '*But* the Devil's Kitchen wasn't formed naturally. It was a deliberate act of God.'

'A deliberate act of God?' Ruth said, teasing him.

'Hey, hear me out. The Roman armies were advancing through Snowdonia. So the local druids decided to climb Pen yr Ole Wen, which is the "Mountain of the White Light". They prayed that God would somehow save them from the Roman invasion. They prayed to the gods of the sun and the moon for three days and three nights. On the fourth day, a bolt of lightning struck the mountain and split it clean in half. Out of the newly formed chasm came this thick fog and cloud. It covered the whole of Snowdonia for weeks and weeks. And the Roman invasion had to stop because of poor visibility. That was as far as they got into Wales before they turned back to England,' Nick said with a satisfied nod.

'That's a good story,' Ruth smiled.

'Well, it would be, except that the appearance of mist on the Devil's Kitchen is now a terrible omen that danger is coming,' Nick said in a spooky voice.

'You don't believe all that nonsense, do you?' Ruth said.

'No, I'm just trying to scare you,' Nick said with a laugh, and then pointed in the other direction. 'That camera is over this way. Come on.'

They walked over the gravel and the tarmac driveway to the right of the house, and then towards a double garage.

'Why do they need a garage?' Ruth asked, thinking out loud.

'I guess people come here and end up staying months, if they're in Witness Protection or awaiting trial,' Nick said.

Ruth looked around. 'There are worse places to be stuck. Better than the safe houses we had in Catford and Peckham. They were right dumps.'

'That's Special Branch and the spooks for you. A better class of safe house,' Nick joked.

It was getting cold, and Ruth regretted not putting on her coat. She fished a packet of ciggies from her pocket, pulled one out and then lit it, shielding the flame of her lighter from the swirling breeze. She took a long, deep drag and immediately felt ten times better. *How the hell am I ever meant to give up smoking when it makes me feel this good?* Nick must have had the same thoughts about booze at one point – although booze was a lot more destructive and chaotic than nicotine.

As Ruth took another drag of her cigarette, she watched as Nick strolled along the front of the garage until he could see the CCTV camera. 'Found it,' Nick said, pointing up to a smart, new-looking dome-shaped camera.

'State-of-the-art ... Anything blocking it?' Ruth asked.

'Nope,' Nick said as he walked directly under where it had been positioned. 'But, have a look at this, boss.'

Ruth joined Nick under the camera. She was a little concerned by his tone of voice. 'What's wrong?'

'I'm not an expert, but I'm pretty sure this wire has been cut,' Nick said.

Ruth looked up. The black wire that went from the CCTV into the brickwork, and then presumably into the house, was hanging down.

'Perhaps it has just come loose from somewhere? Do we need to worry?' Ruth proffered.

Nick shrugged and shook his head. 'The rest of it still looks intact, so it probably just got caught on something and was ripped out of the box. I doubt its anything to worry about. There are cameras everywhere. This place is like Fort Knox.'

CHAPTER 8

4.45 pm

NICK WALKED INTO THE kitchen and put the kettle on. The air still smelled a little stale. He had just been to check on Abu Habib and take him his small bag of possessions, after having searched them thoroughly. He knew that they would have been searched in HMP Rhoswen, but you couldn't be too careful. There were just a few clothes, a couple of books, and a copy of the Koran.

Placing a mug and teabag on the countertop, he waited for the kettle to boil – Abu had requested black tea. Nick was preoccupied with thoughts of Amanda and the coming birth. It was difficult to think about anything else. He was trying to remain positive, but there were moments when his mind would take him to all the things that could go wrong.

It was almost dark outside. Nick pushed the button on the kitchen wall that lowered the shutters. They clicked into action and dropped slowly into place. It was all very high tech. Like something out of a Bond film. If Nick's thoughts weren't on his impending fatherhood, he would have been roaming the house playing with all the gadgets.

Stirring the mug, Nick put the hot teabag in a bin that slid out from under the work surface. PC Garrow had offered to take it up to Abu, but Nick was keen to keep busy. If he kept himself occupied, then the time until he could leave would go quickly.

As Nick walked up the stairs, his thoughts turned to their prisoner, Abu Habib. This was a man who was willing to blow himself into a million pieces in the name of his god. His intention was to murder dozens of innocent bystanders because they refused to believe in the same god as he did.

As far as Nick could see, there seemed little point labelling men like Abu as evil or insane. Their barbaric actions weren't carried out because of some kind of mental illness. That was far too simple. MI5 and Special Branch needed to continue to address and understand the root causes of extremism. That was true of any crime. The *why* was always more important than the *how* or the *when*; that way they could stop it happening again.

Reaching the landing, Nick walked along the corridor and looked through the reinforced window at the centre of the holding cell's security door. The window had wire mesh inlaid in the glass to prevent it from shattering or breaking under great stress. The wire was criss-crossed – it reminded Nick of the old board that he used to play draughts on with his Uncle Mike. The whole door was also flame and heat retardant, which would slow the passage of a house fire.

Abu was sitting on the bed, reading. Nick punched in the code, waited for the electronic beep, opened the door and went in. The door closed behind him with a metallic clunk. Electronically controlled steel deadbolts ran the length of the door. The hinge side of the door was reinforced with more thick bolts and wraparound panels of steel.

'Here's your tea,' Nick said, putting the mug on the bedside table. He wasn't sure how anyone could drink black tea. It just made your mouth furry and your teeth filmy. No thanks.

Abu looked up. 'Thank you.'

Nick noticed that where Abu was holding his book, a nasty, deep scar ran down all five knuckles of his left hand. *Looks like a nasty wound. I wonder how he got that?* He could ask, but he wanted to keep the evening as simple as possible so he could just go home.

He wandered over to the window and looked out.

The garden was a maze of shadows and darkness. A single light from the ground floor threw a feeble vanilla-coloured shape onto the patio. Nick cupped his hands as his eyes adjusted to the gloom. The window smelled of mildew and damp. To the back of the garden, he could make out the black trunks of the trees whose branches spiked up into the sky.

Suddenly, Nick flinched away from the glass as the entire back garden was flooded in light.

What the hell caused that?

The blurred outlines now stood in sharp contrast to the dark elongated shadows of trees and hedges that stretched across the lawn. Something – or someone – had set off the motion sensors.

Nick's stomach tightened.

Cupping his hands on the glass again, his eyes roamed the garden, looking for whatever had triggered the security lights. The smooth sweep of the lawn was clear, as was the patio area closest to the house where there were chairs, a table, and a large wooden gazebo. Scanning away from the house, Nick peered into the impenetrable darkness of the forest. Anyone, or anything, could be in there.

'Problem?' Abu asked, looking up from his book.

Nick ignored him. The lights then went out and the whole scene was plunged back into darkness. For a second, Nick thought he saw someone moving in the trees, but it could have been his eyes playing tricks on him.

A second later, the lights burst into life again. Nick's eye was drawn to movement beside a long, narrow hedge to the left. A copper fox scuttled across the corner of the lawn into the undergrowth and then disappeared into the banks of fir and spruce trees.

'Don't worry. Just a fox,' Nick said, in a tone that implied, '*Don't get your hopes up.*' But he slowly let out his held breath, hoping Abu hadn't noticed.

Looking up into the inky sky, Nick could see the moon was low. It had an almost imperceptible rose-coloured hue. He had heard on the radio that tonight there would be a supermoon. It was explained as the point at which the moon is closest to the earth in the yearly cycle. It would be 20,000 miles closer than usual. It was also known as a 'blood moon' for its reddish appearance. The folklore of North Wales saw it as a symbol of bad luck. The tale told of how the all-powerful moon, a symbol of light and tranquillity, had suffered a vicious attack, and as a result had blood smeared across its face.

Great! Maybe tonight wasn't the best night of the year to be stuck in a safe house in the middle of nowhere. He consoled himself with the thought that the MI5 agents would arrive soon, and he could get back to Llancastell and see Amanda. He felt the muscles in his face soften into the beginnings of a smile at that thought.

Turning to go, Nick looked at Abu. 'Your name is Abu, is that right?'

'Abu, yes,' Abu said.

There would be some police officers who would be irritated that Nick had entered into a conversation with someone like Abu Habib. He was a barbaric terrorist and not to be given the time of day. But to Nick, all criminals were human. He wanted to know what made them tick. The more he understood, the better he would be at his job.

'Let me ask you a question, Abu,' Nick said.

Abu raised an eyebrow and put down his book, *Kashf ush-Shubuhaat – Removal of the Doubts.*

'Please ...' Abu said, gesturing for Nick to continue.

'In the days leading up to your planned bombing in Manchester, did you never think of the innocent people that you would kill? The women and the children?' Nick asked.

'No,' Abu said without hesitation.

'No?' Nick asked with a frown.

'Let me ask you about Syria. Fifteen thousand innocent Muslim civilians have been killed by allied air strikes,' Abu said. 'Do you think about that before you sleep at night?'

'I'm not directly responsible for the deaths in Syria. You would be directly responsible for those that would have died in Manchester,' Nick said.

'You voted for the government of this country, which makes that just semantics,' Abu said.

'Actually, I didn't vote for the current British government ... So, it's just about revenge then?' Nick asked with genuine curiosity.

'No. These acts are a response to the need to defend our Muslim Ummah. I am fighting to protect the Islamic community across the world,' Abu said.

'But you're not from Syria. You're from Hemel Hempstead,' Nick said.

'That's just geography. When thirty British people were killed in Port El Kantaoui in Tunisia, did you not feel outrage?' Abu asked.

'Yes, but they were British citizens on holiday,' Nick said.

'The people killed in Syria are from all around the world. But they are Muslims. They are my people. And so, like you, I feel outrage when they are murdered from the sky,' Abu explained.

'But I don't feel the need to murder innocent people in revenge,' Nick said.

'War is war. The British people must be careful of hypocrisy. You have blood on your hands. In the Second World War, your planes bombed the German city of Dresden. In the resulting firestorm, twenty-five thousand innocent civilians perished terribly. And yet you erect a statue in London to celebrate a war criminal, Sir Arthur Harris, the man who led the attack,' Abu said.

For a moment, Nick could see there was a certain logic to what Abu had said. He had never been comfortable about some of the bombing tactics in the Second World War, but it was before he was born.

'Are you a religious man?' Abu asked.

'Difficult one. I'm not religious in any formal or dogmatic way. But I do believe there is a greater force, a higher power, within the universe that is way beyond my understanding. That force is a positive one and gives us a sense of morality,' Nick said, forming his thoughts as he spoke.

Abu nodded. 'An interesting summation. But the reason that I, and my brothers, are so misunderstood is that we have a resolute, unwavering faith in our god. There is no inkling of doubt that if we follow Allah's teachings, carrying out his message, that we will be rewarded when we die. And that gives us such a powerful certainty that death holds no fear for us. It's something a secular Western society cannot understand.'

'You're right. I don't understand that. And I think we'll have to agree to disagree,' Nick said. He had enjoyed the intellectual jousting of their conversation.

'Thank you for the tea,' Abu said as he picked up his book again. 'And thank you for the conversation.'

Nick opened the door, stepped out, and pushed it closed behind him. He glanced in to see that Abu had returned to reading his book. It was naïve to think that anything he said would have an impact on a man like that. And Abu had explained clearly why that was.

Coming down the stairs, Nick wondered when he would be free to go. Maybe he should ring Amanda to check that everything was all right. But that might just annoy her, he thought, especially if she was trying to get some sleep. This had evaded her lately as the baby had been keeping her up at night with their kicking. She'd ring if there was anything to report.

Popping his head into the surveillance room, Nick saw that Ruth was still sitting at the desk where he had left her. She was pouring over some files. As she turned over a page and rubbed her eyes, he could see she was tired. The events of a week ago had taken their toll on her.

Ruth's phone was quietly playing *Simon and Garfunkel's Greatest Hits* – 'The Sound of Silence'.

'Nice song,' Nick said, listening to the intricate harmonies between Art Garfunkel and Paul Simon's voices.

'It seemed apt. I'm loving how quiet this place is. Beats the noise and smell of our CID office,' Ruth said.

'If you want to experience real noise and smell, just go downstairs to Uniform. It's like a naughty classroom some-times.' Nick chuckled.

'Trumpton,' Ruth said.

'Sorry?' Nick said with a frown. He had no idea what she had just said.

'The children's telly programme *Trumpton*. That's what we used to call the Uniform offices at Peckham nick.' Ruth gestured to her phone. 'Drake rang.'

'What did he say?' Nick asked, hopeful that he would leave for Llancastell soon.

'Greene and Cavendish, the MI5 field agents, will be here in half an hour,' Ruth explained.

'Sounds like an estate agent's ...' Nick said with a smile. 'That's good news ...'

'Then Drake will come down here tomorrow morning to offer a bit of moral support. But as soon as Mr and Mrs MI5 arrive, I want you in that car and back home,' Ruth said.

'Yes, boss,' Nick said. He wasn't about to argue.

'How is our little friend upstairs?' Ruth asked.

'Interesting conversation, but the world is black and white to him. And that makes him very dangerous,' Nick replied.

'Scary stuff, isn't it? I'm looking through his file. I'm at a loss to find out where it went so wrong. Both his parents were teachers at the local secondary school. Reading between the lines, they were *Guardian*-reading socialists, but nothing more than that.'

'Maybe he was rebelling against all that liberal, caring understanding,' Nick suggested.

'By blowing people to pieces? Jesus!' Ruth looked back down at the file. 'First-class degree from Leeds Uni,' she said, thumbing through more pages.

'That's the current profile though, isn't it? Economically comfortable, middle class, well educated, politically and spiritually frustrated. The unofficial analysis of this type of terrorist is that they need to be intelligent enough to understand the complexities of radical Islamic ideology ...' Nick said.

Ruth nodded. 'But impressionable enough to believe them.'

'And then die for them. That's the scary combination,' Nick said.

Ruth frowned as she looked inside her coat. 'You haven't seen my glasses, have you?'

Nick shook his head. 'Nope, sorry. You hate wearing your glasses.'

'I know. But the print on this is tiny. They must be in the car. Or maybe by the garage when I took out my ciggies. Would you be a dear and get them for me?'

'Keys?' Nick said.

'The car's not locked,' Ruth said.

Nick went to go, stopped, and then looked back at Ruth.

'I've got something to ask you,' Nick said, looking a little awkward.

'That sounds ominous,' Ruth said, stopping what she was reading and raising an eyebrow.

'No, nothing bad. It's just that me and Amanda were talking. And when this baby is eventually born, we'd like it if you would be their godmother ... If that's okay with you?' Nick said.

'If that's okay with me? Really?' Ruth asked, wide-eyed. Nick could see how happy she was.

'Yeah, of course,' Nick said, smiling at her.

'It would be an honour. And if we weren't on duty in a safe house with a terrorist, then I would come and give you a big hug,' Ruth said with a grin.

Nick laughed. 'Brilliant. Amanda will be made up.'

Nick's phone buzzed. It was Amanda. 'Speak of the devil. I'd better take this, it's Amanda.'

'Send my love,' Ruth said as she went back to looking through the documents.

'Hiya,' Nick said, and gestured to Ruth that he was going outside to go to the car. 'Everything all right?' He could feel the anxiety build. Why was she ringing?

'Erm ... My waters broke,' Amanda explained.

'What?' Nick stopped in his tracks. It took a second to take in what she had said. 'Shit! Right. When?'

'About five minutes ago. You okay?' Amanda asked.

'Not really. Your waters broke and I'm thirty miles away,' Nick said.

'Don't freak out, you bell-end. It just means that my contractions will probably start soon, that's all. But it could take twelve, even twenty-four hours. It's not like in the films where your waters break, towels and hot water, and ten minutes later your baby pops out,' Amanda said, laughing.

Nick vaguely remembered this. 'Oh yeah. I knew that. But I should be close by from now on.'

Nick went out of the front security door and left it slightly ajar – he didn't have the keys or the code to get back in. Walking down the stone steps of the house, he went across the drive and over to the Astra.

'When are you coming home?' Amanda asked. Nick could tell that she was concerned, despite all her calm, amusing bravado.

'I can leave here in about an hour.' Nick glanced at his watch. 'I'll be home before seven. Promise.'

Nick felt relieved at the thought of getting back to her soon.

'That's fine. Don't worry, nothing will happen tonight,' Amanda said reassuringly.

We don't know that for sure, but I won't say anything, Nick thought to himself.

He opened the car door and began rummaging inside and in the glove compartment for Ruth's glasses. He couldn't see them anywhere.

'Okay. I'll call you when I leave here in case you want me to pick anything up,' Nick said, leaning over to the back seat of the car.

'Okay. Love you. And don't worry,' Amanda said.

'Yeah, love you too. I won't be long,' Nick said as he hung up. Amanda's words had done little to reassure him that she wouldn't go into labour tonight. Now that he knew it had all begun, his adrenaline was racing, and he wasn't even the one giving birth. He inhaled a deep breath and took one last scan of the car. *Don't know what she's talking about. There aren't any glasses in here,* Nick thought to himself.

Slamming the car door shut, Nick made his way over to the garage. His head was swirling with thoughts. Maybe he could have a word with Ruth and head back to Llancastell now. Although, that would mean going against Drake's orders. If anything happened, and he wasn't there, they could both lose their jobs. Not such a brilliant idea. But still. He was having a baby – his first baby. He didn't want to miss anything.

Oh my God, I'm going to be a dad. How is that possible?

When he looked back to where he had been two years earlier, the change seemed remarkable. Back then, Nick was a functioning alcoholic. He would drink from the time he woke to the time he passed out at night. He had been in and out of detox centres and meetings of Alcoholics Anonymous for a decade or more. Nothing seemed to work. He knew that was because he didn't really want to stop drinking. Alcohol was his solution to everything. If he felt anxious, angry, sad, happy, he would pour drink on it. He had become too frightened to feel anything. But he was over two years sober. And that was a bloody miracle.

Nick got to the garage and scanned the area around the faulty security camera where Ruth might have dropped her glasses. Nothing here either.

Glancing to his left, he noticed that the large, sliding garage door was raised by about eighteen inches.

Strange. I thought that was closed when we came and looked at the CCTV camera earlier?

There was no way that he and Ruth would not have noticed that the garage door was not closed properly. Would they? Maybe they were so busy looking up at the CCTV camera, they missed it? No. They were both a bit distracted at that moment, but they were still police officers. It was too obvious for them to have missed, wasn't it?

Crouching down, Nick looked at the gap. The gap was small, but what made Nick wary was that it was high enough for someone to get underneath. He should go back and check with Ruth before doing anything. He hesitated. But he didn't want to put the team on high alert and screw up getting home in time for Amanda. He'd take just a quick look - it had probably just been left unlocked and had opened in the wind.

Standing up, he used the flat of his hands to see if he could push the metal garage door back down to fully closed. It wouldn't budge. So it hadn't just been nudged open by the wind. But perhaps it was fully electronic. *Maybe something had happened when the power was off? Maybe that's why the door had opened?*

Right. I'd better look inside, Nick thought.

Taking out the small Maglite torch from his pocket, he got onto his knees and then looked under the door into the gloomy interior of the garage. It was hard to see from this angle with his body pressed to the ground. On the far side, lines of boxes were stacked on top of each other alongside an old tarpaulin and a workbench. But he couldn't really see much. He'd have to go in.

Rolling onto his back, he shuffled under the garage door and into the large double garage. The ground was cold as he inched inside.

The floor of the garage was smooth concrete. Peering into the darkness, Nick could hardly see anything – the Maglite wasn't strong enough to light up the space effectively. Instead, the high stacks of boxes cast elongated shadows across the floor and walls.

Now he was out of the wind and the noise of birds, Nick noticed the uneasy silence. He stopped and held his breath as he strained to listen. Was that the sound of movement? Then a faint metallic bang. It seemed to come from a long way away, so was probably the gate on its hinges or something similar, but it had done little to dispel the disquiet in his gut. He didn't want to be in this dark garage for a moment longer than necessary.

He moved slowly to his right, hoping he didn't trip on a random box.

There's got to be a light switch somewhere, Nick thought as he waved the beam of his torch over a nearby wall.

A white double light switch appeared in the light of the torch.

Bingo!

Nick clicked the switches down. There was the momentary flashing of strip lights before they burst into life.

Glancing around the garage, he noted that everything seemed to be in order. Gardening tools, boxes of wire, pots of paint, and electronics for the numerous gadgets in the house. But in the corner, something looked out of place.

Clicking off his torch, Nick moved cautiously towards the other side of the garage. Whilst the rest of it was piled high with boxes, there was a conspicuous space at the back where he could see a five-foot steel stepladder set up on the floor. He looked up to the ceiling above where the ladder had been placed. Someone had moved two square ceiling panels to reveal a sizeable gap just big enough for a person to fit through. Even though he had no idea when the panels had been removed, he was concerned. *Looks like someone has climbed up into whatever is above this ceiling,* Nick thought.

Standing on the ladder, Nick clicked on his torch again. He climbed to the top, feeling the ladder wobble under his weight.

He grabbed the nearest ceiling panel to steady himself before standing on tiptoe to look into the darkness. Moving his torch around, he could see that there was a long, narrow space under the rafters. There was a large silver cylindrical tube leading up to a six-foot square vent in the roof, presumably to take any carbon monoxide fumes out of the garage. However, the vent had been removed. There was now a large hole leading out onto the garage roof. From what Nick could remember, the garage was attached to the main body of the house.

Shit! This is not good. His thoughts started racing as he began to connect the dots. *Someone has come through the garage to get onto the roof, with easy access to the safe house. Is that why the wire to the camera over the garage had been cut?*

With his pulse thudding, Nick knew he needed to get back inside to warn Ruth about what he had found. Even though there was a part of him that said he was being overcautious – and Amanda would kill him later if it amounted to nothing – he would still flag it up.

He climbed down the stepladder, jogged across the garage, got onto the floor and rolled under the garage door. He stood up, ran across the drive and headed for the front door. His adrenaline was starting to kick in. Was someone really trying to break into the safe house? Or was he being paranoid?

Bounding up the stone steps, Nick found that the front door was now closed. Whether taken by the wind, or been purposely shut, it didn't matter. He needed the code to get inside, but Ruth had it.

Fuck! This is getting worse.

He banged on the door, then realised that no one inside would hear. It was made from reinforced steel. Ruth was probably still in the surveillance room listening to music.

Now what?

Nick pulled out his phone. He would ring her and get her to let him in. If he was right about some kind of intruders, then Ruth needed to unlock the armoury compartment in the car so they could get the handguns to protect themselves.

Holding up the phone, Nick could see that he wasn't getting any signal from the house. Why not? Why is there no Wi-Fi? They were in the middle of nowhere, so there was no hope of 4G!

The signal had been working fine earlier, but now nothing. A sickening thought occurred to Nick. *What if the broadband signal had been purposefully cut so we can't ring for help?*

With no signal, Nick knew he had no way of getting in contact with Ruth.

What about the Tetra police radio in the Astra? However, if his smartphone didn't work out there, he didn't hold out much hope for the rather archaic Tetra radio, which was part walkie-talkie, part eighties Nokia brick.

Nick jogged over, went around the car, opened the driver's door. He grabbed the Tetra radio from the dashboard.

'Control from three-six, are you reading me, over?' Nick said, praying that somehow his signal would be picked up by the CAD operator in Llancastell.

Nothing.

He pressed the button again. 'Three-six to control, this is an emergency.'

Please, please, someone pick this up.

Nothing. All he could hear was the crackle of static.

Taking two steps back, Nick looked up at the safe house. Ruth and PC Garrow were inside, and a person or persons were trying to get in ... Or were already inside.

Nick went to close the driver's door, but he spotted the front tyre of the Astra. It was flat. He glanced nervously at the back tyre on that side. It was the same. Flat as a pancake.

Jesus Christ! Someone's punctured the tyres. Now what? Maybe I can attract Ruth's attention from the back of the house, Nick thought, as he sprinted quickly towards the garage. Heart thumping, he knew that his only chance to get round the back was to follow the route that the intruders had taken.

There was no question about it now as Nick steadied his resolve. They were under attack – and he had to let Ruth know.

CHAPTER 9

5.27 pm

RUTH LOOKED AT HER watch and frowned. Nick had been gone for nearly fifteen minutes in his quest to find her glasses. Where could he be? Maybe he was still talking to Amanda? She hoped everything was all right. There was no way she could allow Nick to miss the birth of his child. These days it was virtually unheard of for fathers not to be present at the birth. When Ruth was born in 1969, her dad spent the whole of the labour and delivery in the pub across the road from St Thomas' Hospital in Westminster with his brothers. When he turned up to see her as a baby, the nurses wouldn't let him in until he'd sobered up.

Those were the bloody days, eh? Ruth thought.

Getting up from the table in the surveillance room, Ruth wandered out into the hallway to see if she could find Nick. Even though she had been tired, she now had a little bit of a spring in her step. She couldn't believe that Nick and Amanda had invited her to be their new baby's godmother. She had never been asked before. She wondered if they would have a proper religious christening. A church, the prayers, water from the font over the baby's head. And that slightly unnerving part about renouncing the Devil and all his followers. Maybe that was just Catholics? Or that scene from *The Godfather* where loads of people got shot at the same time? She couldn't remember now.

Even though Ruth had been told she had been christened in a church close to Clapham Common, she had never seen any photographic evidence. Neither had her younger brother Chris of his supposed christening at the same church. They used to joke that their parents had made the christenings up to save money. Ruth didn't even think she had met her own godparents. They were old drinking mates of her dad, and they seemed to lose touch as Ruth grew up. She resolved that she would try to be a decent godmother. Birthdays, presents and maybe the odd word of advice.

But where the bloody hell is Nick?

Strolling into the living area, Ruth spotted PC Garrow sitting quietly, reading a book.

'Any good?' Ruth asked.

'Not really. Picked it up off the shelf over there. Some crime thriller thing. Someone's chopped up a body and sent it all over the world. Bit far-fetched, you know?' PC Garrow replied, sitting up at Ruth's appearance at the doorway. He gestured to his phone. 'Think there's something wrong with the Wi-Fi? It went off about ten minutes ago. And there's no 4G out here, obviously.'

'Right. We're in the middle of who-knows-where, so I don't suppose broadband speed is up to much.' Ruth noticed a graze on his wrist where he had been cuffed to Abu Habib. 'Not nice, being handcuffed to a suspect, is it?' Ruth said, sitting down on the arm of a sofa.

PC Garrow shrugged. 'Part of the job. In the long term, I'd prefer more of a challenge.'

Ruth nodded. 'Christ, I remember the first time I hand-cuffed someone to me. I was still at Lavender Hill in South London, so this must have been twenty-five years ago. Me and my sergeant were chasing after a car that had been reported stolen. We followed the car into some crappy, old car park on the Portchester Estate and the driver crashed into a concrete post. The passenger did a runner, so my sergeant went after him. He told me to see if the driver was all right. Then cuff him until another unit arrived. So, I went over to the driver, Shayne Townsend his name was, and he looks up at me. And I ask Shayne if he needs an ambulance. He tells me that if I'm going to try to arrest him, then I'm going to need an ambulance. He gets out of the car, and I realise that Shayne is about six foot six and built like a brick shit house. Covered in tattoos, long before everyone had tattoos. But before he can say anything else, I've cuffed him to me. Shayne goes mad. He's gonna kill me if I don't take them off. I say my sarge has got the keys. It's Met Police policy. So he says, right, you're coming with me. And Shayne drags me off my feet as we go. I can't get my balance,' Ruth said with a smile.

'Jesus, how did you get out of that?' PC Garrow asked.

'He's dragging me through the side streets. Eventually we stop. My wrist is cut to pieces. Shayne says he's going to get a hacksaw to get the cuffs off. And I'm trying to call for back-up. I spot a transit van that's parked beside us. So I quickly take the cuff off my wrist and clamp it around the door handle of this van,' Ruth said.

PC Garrow was sitting upright and laughing.

'Shayne is doing his nut. Except I didn't spot there's someone in the van. They drive off with Shayne handcuffed to their passenger door. And Shayne goes bouncing down the road. Broken arm, ribs, fractured cheek. I eventually get him to A&E at St George's. Then Shayne asks me out for a drink. He says I'm pretty fit for a copper,' Ruth said, chortling.

PC Garrow pulled a face and chuckled. 'That's hilarious. Never boring. That's what everyone told me when I joined the force.'

'Nope. Never a dull moment ... I used to have friends who would tell me how they would sit at work, watching the clock and waiting for it to get to five. It's never like that for us, is it Jim?'

'No, ma'am. The days fly by.'

'You know your most important skill?' Ruth asked him.

'No, ma'am,' he said, shaking his head.

'Instinct. Your gut. What they called in the old days your "copper's nose". If it doesn't feel right, if something feels "off", then nine times out of ten it is. DNA, profiling, satellites, drones, they're all useful. But I trust my instinct first,' Ruth said, hoping she wasn't coming across as patronising.

'Yes, ma'am. Thank you,' PC Garrow said.

'Speaking of which, have you seen DS Evans?' Ruth asked.

'No, ma'am. Not for a while ... I checked on the prisoner ten minutes ago. He's asleep on the bed upstairs,' he answered. 'I'm about to make a coffee if you fancy one?'

Ruth smiled at him. 'Yeah, ta. That would be lovely, Jim. I'm looking through some stuff in the surveillance room ... And if you see DS Evans, can you redirect him my way? He's meant to be bringing me my glasses.'

Ruth turned to go but was halted by a hollow noise. It sounded like movement from upstairs.

'Did you hear something?' Ruth asked.

PC Garrow frowned and shook his head. 'No, ma'am. Nothing.'

Bloody hell. This place is getting to me. I must be imagining things, Ruth thought.

Going out into the hallway, she stopped and listened again. Nothing.

Satisfied that everything was okay, Ruth walked back across the hallway and into the surveillance room. She wanted to read the article that Stephen Flaherty had attached to the email he'd sent to her earlier.

Ruth sat down on the sofa, opening her phone and downloading the file, before pulling up the article. It was a piece from a tabloid newspaper.

The dark secrets of London's Secret Garden sex parties that led to 'orgy' scandals and a 'murder' mystery.

Popping champagne and posing in bikinis, a harem of stunning models from around the world was pictured partying the night away in the latest offering from the Secret Garden, an elite sex party for the great, the good and the beautiful.

However, the reputation of these extravagant and discrete soirees, thrown by millionaire hedge fund manager Jamie Parsons, has been darkening in recent months, with claims of everything from satanic rituals, underage sex, and the mysterious death of a Portuguese model.

While Parsons describes the parties as no more sordid than a stag do in Magaluf, guests describe drugs, orgies, sadomasochism and dangerous role play. A source we spoke to, a 23-year-old model from Dublin, claimed she was paid to take part in a sex game with two well-known British politicians. She was asked to dress up as a schoolgirl and refer to one of the men as 'Daddy'. The model claimed that there were men at these parties willing to part with thousands of pounds to sleep with teenagers dressed as nurses. A well-known music industry figure passed around a statue of the Greek god Priapus, which had a very large phallus, and asked the women there to perform oral sex on it while he masturbated.

The party was rocked two years ago by scandal with the suspicious death of the Portuguese model, Beatriz Santos. There were rumours that Santos was planning a tell-all book exposing the Secret Garden parties and 'naming names'. Santos was found dead at her Kensington flat, but the post-mortem and coroner recorded that she had died from natural causes. Her family claimed that Santos had been poisoned and that her body and neck had been covered in bruises. They paid for a private post-mortem, but the results were inconclusive. The coroner said he was satisfied with the original verdict.

Ruth sat back. Had the decadent and sleazy goings-on at the Secret Garden parties played any part in why Sarah had gone missing? Of course, it might be a red herring. However, Ruth's instinct was that there was something sinister about the events.

The thought that there was a darker side to Sarah overwhelmed her. Ruth had thought that this wasn't Sarah's scene at all – she'd had her wild moments, but nothing quite like this – but after her recent revelations with Jamie Parsons, Ruth wasn't sure she knew the real Sarah anymore. She couldn't help but feel bitter knowing that Sarah wanted more than her, but she couldn't pin down what it was. Maybe it was the secrecy and the darkness that Sarah was attracted to?

Glancing down at the time on the bottom of the phone screen, Ruth could see that she had about fifteen minutes before the spooks arrived. She had time to go out the back and have a ciggie.

The last time she'd had any meaningful dealings with MI5 was when an IRA cell had been discovered in Peckham in 1997. Having raided a flat behind Peckham High Street, Ruth and her officers had discovered nearly forty Semtex explosive devices. The papers and maps they found with them indicated that the IRA had planned a series of attacks on electricity substations that would have knocked out a huge part of the national grid and plunged London and much of South East England into darkness. MI5 and Special Branch were called in and, once the police had handed over the evidence, they took the lead on the case. Ruth had found the various members of MI5 a 'cold bunch'. Meticulous, well educated, but lacking the emotion or humour of the Met.

Taking her coat from the back of the chair, Ruth thought she would have a smoke and a scoot around for Nick. As she went out into the hallway, she patted her coat pocket to check that the ciggies and lighter were there.

Making her way to the back of the safe house, she found a security door that led out into the back-garden area. There didn't seem to be any heating here, and it was freezing. She looked at the code pad. She had memorised the number.

Ruth was just about to type the numbers in when she was blinded by a sudden explosion of light in the garden. She squinted outside through the large reinforced windows.

Obviously a motion sensor had triggered the security lights. The wind, or those damned bats again, or something. It had made Ruth jump out of her skin. Sitting in this house in the middle of nowhere had her nerves on edge. She'd be glad to get home to a glass of wine – if only those spooks would hurry up and get here.

Just in case, Ruth moved forward towards the glass. She peered cautiously outside.

Could have been a cat or an animal?

The light dropped again as the motion sensor switched off.

But not a moment later, the garden was flooded with light again, and where previously was just an empty lawn, a shadowy figure stood.

Ruth shrieked and jumped away from the window.

The figure was backlit. Ruth couldn't see anything but the outline of a person standing there.

Although she couldn't see their eyes, she could feel their stare boring into her. She took another step back from the door, wishing she hadn't left her firearm in the car.

She was about to turn and run when the figure stepped into the light. It was Nick.

For fuck's sake, you dick head!

'You scared the shit out of me, you silly bugger!' Ruth shouted, as she went to the security door to let him inside. 'What are you doing out there? Auditioning for a horror movie?' Ruth punched the numbers into the keypad. The lights turned red and let out a flat, staccato beep. 'Stupid technology.' Ruth looked up and gestured to the security box. 'Just got to punch in the code.' She emphasised the pronunciation so that Nick could read her lips through the glass.

Nick was motioning to her.

Ruth smiled back at him. 'I'm coming, I'm coming. Keep your wig on.'

However, Nick didn't return her smile. Instead, his eyes were wide with fear and he was yelling something. He was scaring her.

What's he saying?

Then the realisation hit her.

Her blood ran cold.

Ruth turned and saw a tall, broad figure looming over her, silhouetted in the ceiling light. She felt a sickening thud on the side of her head and everything went black.

CHAPTER 10

5.33 pm

NICK WATCHED IN HORROR as Ruth fell to the ground unconscious. He darted out of the range of the garden lights, hoping that he hadn't been seen. His heart was thudding. He needed to think.

Now what do I do?

The man he had seen inside was South Asian and dressed in dark clothes. Had he spotted Nick outside? Was it just this one man? How many men were there? What were they going to do with Ruth? How had they arrived at the property undetected? Were they armed?

Each question raced through Nick's head. He didn't have the answer to any of them. His head was swimming.

Focus on what you do *know,* Nick thought.

He needed to get inside to help Ruth. That was his priority. But where was PC Garrow? It would be safe to assume that whoever the man who attacked Ruth was, he was here for Abu Habib. However, he, and any accomplices, would need the code to open the security door on Abu's holding cell. Ruth was the only one with the code. And now she was unconscious. God knows what they'd do to get the code from her.

Nick regained his composure. And remembered his conversation with Habib earlier in the evening. *Fuck them, they can have him for all I care. I'm getting Ruth out of there.*

Breathing hard, Nick edged along the garden wall, keeping in its shadow. He looked at the back wall of the house. On the first floor, he was surprised to see a window that was open by a couple of inches. Why it had been left open, he didn't know, but right now he didn't care. It was too far over to reach from the drainpipe. The only way to get to it would be to swing down from the roof. And that looked too dangerous.

There has to be a better way to get back inside.

Nick knew that he could retrace his route up onto the safe-house roof, across the flat rooftop of the garage, down through the open air vent and out to the front of the house. If only he had the keys to the car, he could get the Glocks out.

Nick pulled at the iron drainpipe to make sure it was secure.

Right, let's do this.

Pulling himself up, he got a footing on a gap in the brick-work. It had been a lot easier coming down, even though he had jumped the last twenty feet and jarred his knee. However, he had enough adrenaline pumping around his body to not feel a thing.

Pushing and pulling, Nick reached a window on the first floor. Grabbing onto the frame, he got a footing on the sill. From here, he could just about make the last few yards up to the roof ...

Suddenly, the wood of the windowsill gave way, disappearing from beneath his feet. The piece of wood fell and hit the gravel below.

His face slammed into the stonework of the building and his legs scrambled in mid-air as he desperately tried to find something to get a foothold on. The muscles and tendons in his hands were burning with the sheer exertion of holding on. He looked down. It had to be a twenty foot drop. He wouldn't survive that without some kind of serious injury.

He glanced right. The guttering? Would it take his weight? He didn't have a choice. If he didn't do something, he was going to lose his grip and plummet. He swung his right leg up. His foot landed between the guttering and the bottom section of the roof. He followed with his other foot so that both his legs could take his bodyweight as he manoeuvred around. He threw his hands up and caught a brick section of the roof. *Nice one.*

With no time to marvel at his Spiderman skills, Nick made progress upwards, scrambling up the steep tiles. He got to the ridge of the roof. Edging along slowly, he reached the section that adjoined the flat top of the garage. With a slight leap, Nick landed with both feet on a solid section of roof. *Bloody hell! That was scary ...*

Sprinting over to the open air vent, Nick climbed inside. It was musty and warm. He dropped into the shaft and crawled along on his elbows. The metal ridges dug into his forearms. He didn't have time to stop for relief. He drove on. A few seconds later, he came to where the panels had been taken off the garage ceiling. Except the garage lights had been turned off. Someone had been in there – or was still in there.

Taking out his torch, Nick paused to listen. Nothing. No sound of movement. He then leant his head down through the square gap in the ceiling. He waved his torch around, looking for any kind of movement.

Nothing again. It was silent.

Dropping down onto the stepladder, Nick descended to the concrete floor of the garage.

To his right, Nick saw a series of storage shelves with gardening tools. There were some old board games, books, and an old box of fireworks. Flipping open the lid, he grabbed a small handful and stuffed them into his pocket. He knew that anything that could create a distraction might be useful.

To his left, he noticed a new-looking sit-down lawnmower. Beside that, several large red cans of petrol. It gave him an idea.

Nick grabbed the first petrol can. It was full. Twisting the top, he poured the contents across the garage floor. Then he grabbed another can and doused the piles of boxes that were stacked against the back wall. The fumes were thick in his nostrils. His eyes watered as he tossed the empty can away.

He knew that if he needed distraction at some point, he could torch the garage if the fireworks didn't work. He went to the partially raised garage door, laid down and rolled under.

Standing up, Nick surveyed the area. How had the intruders arrived? They must have a vehicle somewhere. He needed to find a way inside and get Ruth and PC Garrow out.

Looking up at the large moon in the sky, Nick was grateful for its light. As he came around the main driveway, the whole house loomed in front of him. Whether the intruders were here to kill or rescue Abu Habib, they needed access to the secure holding cell. And they needed the code to get in. Nick had seen the reinforced door – they weren't going to get through that without it. He had to get to Ruth before they tried to force the code out of her.

Out in the fresh air of the driveway, away from the noxious petrol fumes, Nick could smell something different on the breeze. The night freshness was littered with a bitter fragrance he knew all too well. Cigarette smoke. For the briefest of mo-

ments he thought Ruth had got away and was having a casual
ciggie somewhere, waiting for him with a sardonic smile and a
quick witticism. But glancing around he could see no tell-tale
orange glow of a cigarette. Nothing. It could have been coming
from the back of the house – or even inside.

Gazing up at the various windows, Nick was trying to cal-
culate if he could scale the outside of the house and get in
somewhere. He was counting his lucky stars that he'd survived
the scaling of the back of the house. All the windows on this
side of the building also appeared closed and locked. Then he
noticed a thin shard of light running down the side of the front
door.

Bloody hell! It's open.

Nick scanned left and right. But rather than run to his easy
entrance, he was frozen to the spot. *That means someone is out
here. Someone is outside here having a ...*

Bang! Something or someone hit Nick hard.

He went reeling, lost his footing and fell heavily to the
gravel.

Before he could look up, a man was on him, pinning him
to the ground. The man sat on his legs and used his hands to
stop Nick from using his arms.

Nick focussed his eyes. Even in the darkness he could see
the man's dark skin and flashing eyes. Maybe North African?
His face was covered with a thick beard and he wore a dark
woollen hat.

Jesus! This is not good.

The man dropped his elbow down onto Nick's right arm
and reached back with his free arm for something inside his

robe. Then a flash of silver glinted in the moonlight. A serrated hunting knife.

The man was big and strong. For a second, Nick thought he was a goner.

Gritting his teeth, the man said something. Nick didn't understand it, but it was said with such venom that Nick flinched at the projectile spittle that landed on his face as the man spat out the words.

However, as his attacker took his focus away for a second to bring the knife to Nick's neck, the weight pinning down Nick's right leg shifted away. Now was his chance.

With all his strength, Nick smashed his leg into the man's back and side. It knocked his assailant off balance and released Nick's right arm. Nick swivelled hard and used his free limb to throw the man off him and over onto his back.

Leaping to his feet, Nick kicked the man in the jaw as he tried to get up, sending the man's head backwards. Now dazed, the man shook his head. Nick kicked him again with everything he had. A pain shot up his leg. He'd cracked some of his toes on the man's skull.

Spinning around, Nick sprinted away from the house, ignoring the roaring pain in his toes with every step. His heart was pounding. The gravel crunched noisily under his feet. He glanced back, not risking stopping even for a second. The man was back on his feet and giving chase.

He must have a head made of bloody concrete!

Dashing on, Nick hurdled some low bushes, pounded up a steep grass bank and into the cover of tall trees. He was on the edge of the forest – but it was pitch black.

Shielded by the trees, away from the moon and the motion-activated lights of the house, Nick was invisible. Stopping briefly, he squinted back behind him. The man was running full pelt in his direction.

Shit! He was only seconds away.

Darting hard right, Nick began to weave in and out of the trees. A thin branch whipped against his forehead and broke. Ducking, and using his hands to feel his way forward, Nick was making slow progress. However, the growing darkness also gave him the advantage of stealth. Crouching low on his haunches, he tried to get his breath back as quietly as he could. The pulse in his neck thudded rhythmically in his eardrums.

Holding his breath, he craned his neck, trying to listen to where his pursuer had gone. Nothing.

It would be impossible for him to follow Nick into the forest without making any noise.

Nick could feel his hands shaking. It was exertion, the adrenaline, and the fear.

Where the bloody hell is he? Maybe he's turned back to get help?

Holding his breath again, Nick listened. Nothing. Just the soft rustle of leaves.

Suddenly, a beam of light flashed across the forest canopy above, which seemed to throw the part of the forest that he crouched in into daylight.

Bollocks! He's got a torch.

Nick could see it wasn't just a torch. It was a high-powered LED torch.

If the man looked his way, he would see Nick, and if he moved, he would hear him. He was trapped.

Now what?

Looking around, Nick saw a broken branch lying on the leaves. It was about two feet long. He reached out and grabbed it around its girth and dragged it towards him. Every snap and crunch of the wood against the earth sounded deafening in the silence.

The terrorist was getting closer. The white beam of light zipped left and right.

Taking one long deep breath, he clasped the branch in two hands and stood up. Nick didn't care if he was seen or if he made a noise. He had to do something. He wasn't going to spend the night creeping around the forest. He had to get Ruth and PC Garrow out of that place. He had to get back to Amanda.

Ducking past a tree, Nick's feet were noisy on the leaves and the twigs that broke. Half a second later, the beam of light fell directly on him, casting his shadow up into the haunting trees around him like some ghastly shadow-puppet show. He had been spotted.

Nick sprinted for another hundred yards before he saw a thick tree. Darting round the other side of it, he panted, his eyes closed, his toes throbbing, his back pressed hard against its trunk. He brought the heavy branch up to his heaving chest.

The sound of running footsteps was getting closer. Closer. Closer still. From the size and direction of the torchlight, Nick could tell the man was almost upon him.

The noise stopped. The man had halted to look around.

This is it. Time to make my move.

Peeking momentarily from behind the tree, Nick saw the figure of the man in the shadows. He was looking the other way.

Breaking into a sprint, Nick reached him before the man had time to react. As if using a baseball bat, Nick swung the branch with both hands. It *cracked* against the man's head.

Take that, you fucker!

For a second, the man turned and looked at Nick.

Jesus! 'How are you still standing?' he said aloud, incredulous.

Then the man collapsed to the ground. He was unconscious.

'And stay down.'

Dropping to his knees, Nick delved into the man's pockets. There was a cheap burner mobile phone, some plastic ties, and documents.

Finding nothing else useful, Nick hooked the man under his shoulders and dragged him to the nearest tree. He took one of the plastic ties and secured the man's hands behind him and the thin trunk of a tree. He was going nowhere. Taking the small hat from his head, Nick jammed it into the man's mouth. He didn't want him regaining consciousness and shouting out.

Nick needed to get back to Ruth and get her out of there.

Taking the torch and the knife, he jogged back the way he had come. His broken toes were throbbing. There was sweat running down his back and dripping from his forehead. At least he had the torch to light his way.

Coming slowly down the bank, Nick reached the gravel driveway. He turned off the torch so as not to draw attention to himself. The light of the moon illuminated the house.

I wonder how many of them there are? At least they're one man down.

Composing himself, Nick needed to make a plan.

Something to the left caught his eye. Lights on the road leading up to the safe house.

Headlights.

Nick glanced down at his watch. It must be the MI5 agents – they were due any minute. Thank God, reinforcements! Maybe that was them? It had to be. Who else would it be? The headlights looked to be over a mile away still. Maybe two?

At least help was coming, Nick thought. But they would have no idea that there was an attack taking place at the safe house …

Nick needed to get to them and warn them before they reached the house.

CHAPTER 11

5.48 pm

ALL AROUND HER WAS black, but Ruth could hear the low hubbub of voices. Their volume and clarity varied and distorted, as if someone were tuning in and out a radio. Then, just as Ruth thought she was going to come out of her sleep, she would return to the comfort of dreamland. The voices got louder. They were voices of men. A language she couldn't understand. Straining to hear, Ruth couldn't place it.

There was a dull ache in the middle of her head. Like the onset of toothache.

God! It feels like the hangover you get after two bottles of heavy red wine.

Why couldn't she get out of this dream? A dizzy, falling feeling overwhelmed her. It was like being on a rollercoaster – it was making her feel sick.

Trying to stretch, Ruth knew that she couldn't move her arms. There was something very uncomfortable around her wrists. Like they were trapped, or she'd got them caught.

Wake up, Ruth, come on!

Flickering her eyes open, Ruth looked up at the man glaring down at her. He was talking to her. She recognised the language as German. The blue, lifeless eyes, the thin blonde hair and the twisted smirk.

It was Jurgen Kessler.

Kessler was asking her a question. She spotted another man laughing in an armchair on the other side of the room. The man was laughing so hard that he held his stomach.

It was Jamie Parsons.

Where the bloody hell am I? *Ruth thought as she tried to wriggle her wrists free.*

Have Kessler and Parsons kidnapped me or something? What's going on?

Kessler leant forward and kissed her gently on the forehead.

'We're going to make everything all right for you, dearest Ruth,' Kessler said. However, when he moved away from her, she saw that the man was Dan, her ex-husband. He gave her his cheeky wink.

'Stay there and get some rest,' Dan said. 'Unless you want me to fuck you again?'

And with that, Ruth rolled gently back to the darkness.

She could hear the voices again. Then she remembered. Someone had hit her on the head. Nick had tried to warn her. The last thing she could remember was the figure behind her.

Keeping her eyes closed as she began to slowly regain consciousness, Ruth could hear the men talking again. Thick accents. But they were speaking English. '... Yes, *inshallah* ... Habib ...' What were they talking about?

The details of where Ruth was and what she was doing there came flooding back. An MI5 safe house in Snowdonia. Abu Habib was their prisoner. Someone had hit her across the back of the head. She could only assume the men in the room with her had attacked her and tied her up. They were here for Abu Habib.

Ruth was yanked from her thoughts by an icy-cold splash to her face. In a jolt of shock, she opened her eyes, spluttering. A man in his fifties, greying stubble, and a prayer cap looked directly at her. He was holding a large – now empty – glass.

'She's okay,' the man said to another as he moved away.

Blinking her eyes, Ruth could see she was in the surveillance room of the safe house. Trying to move, she was unable to adjust the position of her hands. They'd been secured with something hard that dug into her wrists – plastic ties, she assumed.

The other man in the room was short, muscular, with dark, hooded eyes. 'What do we do with her now?' he asked, gesturing to Ruth.

'Wait until Yasir comes back.'

They all looked up to see a thin, wiry man in his early twenties arrive at the doorway. He looked agitated.

'Where have you been, Kashif?' the short man asked angrily.

'I can't find Yasir anywhere,' Kashif said, making a hand gesture and looking uneasy.

'Don't be ridiculous!' the short man growled, approaching Kashif aggressively.

'Hamzar, keep calm,' the man in his fifties said. He was clearly worried that Hamzar was a loose cannon.

'What about Habib?' Hamzar snapped.

'There's a holding cell on the first floor,' Kashif said fearfully and then gestured to the older man. 'But Sameer is right. There is a code to get in.'

'Did Habib see you?' Sameer asked.

'I don't think so,' Kashif said.

'We need Yasir for the code,' Hamzar grumbled. 'Where could he have gone?'

And where is Nick? Ruth thought. The men had seen him. He had to be somewhere outside. Was that why this Yasir was missing?

'I'll go and look for Yasir again,' Kashif said and disappeared.

Sameer said, 'Yasir went to look for whoever that man was outside.'

Hamzar leaned into Ruth's face. She could smell his stale breath and cigarettes. 'You have a friend here? Who was the man outside?'

Ruth shook her head and furrowed her brow. 'I don't know what you're talking about.' Hamzar slapped Ruth so hard across the right-hand side of the face that she saw stars for a few seconds.

Jesus!

'Don't mess us about or I will slit your throat,' Hamzar said, pulling a twelve-inch machete out of his robe.

Ruth's face stung and her jawbone throbbed – but she wasn't going to confirm that Nick was outside unless she had to.

'What man?' Ruth mumbled, trying to get her breath back.

Grabbing her by the hair, Hamzar jerked Ruth's head backwards and put the machete's sharpened blade to her throat.

'I've never seen him before,' Ruth gasped.

She could feel the cold of the metal. As he pushed the machete against her neck, Ruth could feel the sting as it cut the skin.

He's actually going to kill me, Ruth thought. She felt the trickle of blood run down her neck and onto her chest.

'Okay, okay ... He's my DCI,' Ruth mumbled, praying that Hamzar would move the blade away from her throat. They would have guessed he was a police officer by now.

But where is PC Garrow? She hoped he was all right. Did they know about him too?

'DCI?' Hamzar sneered.

'Detective chief inspector,' Sameer said calmly.

Hamzar withdrew the blade, stepped back and shrugged. 'He's going nowhere. We've slashed your tyres.'

Shit. If they managed to get out, there was no way they could use the police car to escape. The intruders must have got here somehow ... But the MI5 agents were on their way. What time was it anyway? How long had she been out for? Maybe they were already here ...

Sameer walked towards Ruth. 'You brought Abu Habib here, yes?'

Ruth nodded, her mind still whirring. 'Yes.'

'So, you have the code for the cell?' Sameer said.

Ruth shook her head. 'No, I don't. My DCI has the code. He's the senior ranking officer and the only person with access to the security codes.'

Ruth hoped that they had bought her explanation. The code was on her phone in her pocket.

'She's lying,' growled Hamzar.

'Just leave it,' Sameer said. 'Why would they give her the code? She's just the babysitter. Yasir will be back soon and he has the code.'

Sameer was obviously keen to pacify Hamzar.

'Then we have no use for this bitch,' Hamzar said, pointing to Ruth. 'It's better that I take her outside and kill her.'

Ruth's stomach lurched with terror.

Sameer shook his head. 'Once we have Abu Habib, you can do what you want with her. But until then, we must wait for Yasir.'

Sameer went over to the bank of CCTV monitors and sat down.

'You see Yasir anywhere?' Hamzar asked.

Sameer shook his head.

'What about this DCI?' Hamzar said.

'Nothing. There's no one anywhere,' Sameer said, gesturing to the monitors.

Kashif appeared at the door. He was breathless and agitated.

'Did you find him?' Hamzar barked at him.

'No, no. He's vanished,' Kashif gasped. 'But there's a car coming.'

'What?' Sameer said, frowning.

The MI5 agents, Ruth thought. *And they're walking straight into a trap.*

'What the hell do you mean a car is coming?' thundered Hamzar.

'I remember from the journey. The road coming up here was a few miles. And I saw the headlights of a car in the distance behind us but thought they were gonna turn off to some farm or something. I didn't think they were coming here,' Kashif said nervously. 'What if they know we're here?'

As Ruth looked at Kashif's anxious, boyish face, something caught her eye moving behind him in the hall. A figure ap-

peared and then disappeared. PC Garrow! The men clearly had
no idea that there was a third police officer. What was he doing?

'No one knows we're here,' Sameer said, trying to calm him.

Ruth wondered if the MI5 agents would be armed. She
thought of the two Glock handguns that were locked in the car
– if only Nick had taken the car keys, he would have had access
to them.

Hamzar pulled a large black kit bag across the floor and
lifted it onto the table. Ruth could see it was heavy. He un-
zipped it. Then he pulled out a Kalashnikov AK-47 machine
gun. Ruth had only ever seen them in photographs, but she
knew they were the terrorists' weapon of choice.

Now that he was holding the gun, Hamzar's body language
changed as he puffed out his chest and walked with a swagger.

*Oh God, he thinks he's in some terrible Sylvester Stallone
film!*

Hamzar checked the chamber, then clicked the curved
black magazine, which held forty bullets, into place.

Ruth caught Sameer's eye for a second. He looked away. If
any of the men seemed uncertain about what they were doing,
she could see it was him. This was useful information. The weak
link.

'Right. Open the gates in about two minutes. Let's go welcome our guests,' Hamzar said, as he snapped back the lever to
load the weapon.

CHAPTER 12

5.43 pm

HAVING SPOTTED THE razor wire that topped the walls of the compound, Nick had to rethink his plan to intercept the MI5 agents approaching the safe house. Instead, he had gone back to the garage and taken the large, dark tarpaulin and a paint-splattered stepladder. Dragging them across the gravel drive, Nick used the torch to find a suitable place to scale the boundary. He needed to get over the wall and intercept the car; if the terrorists saw the car approaching the gates on the CCTV, they might attack. Nick didn't know if the intruders were armed or not, but he would not take that risk.

Looking up at the cameras, he tried to see if there were any blind spots along the wall. He was scared of attracting attention. He picked the point where he thought it least likely that he would be spotted.

Pushing the stepladder against the stone wall, Nick grabbed the tarpaulin. It smelled damp. Holding it in the middle, he flicked the sheet up and over. He hoped the thick waxy canvas would protect him from the razor wire that ran along the top of the wall. He'd folded it over again, just in case.

Pulling on the tarpaulin, Nick could see that it had snagged on the wire – which is exactly what he wanted. He could pull himself up the last six feet of the wall by clutching the canvas.

The old stones of the wall meant that he also had decent footholds.

Compared to the climb up the house itself, it was easy. *A smooth concrete wall would have been far more secure,* he thought to himself. *I mean, who designed this place?*

Pushing himself up, he tentatively pressed down with his hands to check that the thick tarpaulin was acting as protection against the sharp steel of the wire. It had worked a treat.

Nick turned himself around and sat on top of the wall. Gazing back down the wooded hill, he could see the headlights approaching. The car would arrive in less than a minute. The wind picked up and swirled around him. He needed to get help and fast, otherwise he wasn't sure how he was going to rescue Ruth and the young constable. Let alone get home to Amanda. He had no way of contacting her. It was torture. And how were they treating Ruth, locked up in the house? She was the only one who had the information the intruders needed. But had they realised that yet? He didn't want to think about it. He wished he could go striding in and get her out of there. If they had hurt her ... He tried to put the thought out of his head.

How was he going to get out of this?

Take it one step at a time.

Dropping slowly down the other side of the wall, Nick used the tarpaulin and the uneven stone surface to guide his descent. He had no choice but to jump down the last five feet. A white-hot searing pain shot up his foot and leg from his broken toes.

Grimacing, he hobbled down the road. The car came around the bend. Nick waved his hands. The car flashed its headlights, slowed, and then pulled over. He could see a middle-aged man and woman inside. They were white, well-groomed and dressed in smart-casual clothes – they looked like spooks to him.

Getting out his warrant card – thank God he had that on him – Nick leant down as the man, cropped hair, forties and well-built, buzzed down the window. The woman leaned forward slightly so she could see Nick from the passenger seat. With blonde wavy hair, she was attractive, and in different circumstances Nick would have given her a second look – but not today!

'Detective Sergeant Nick Evans, Llancastell CID,' Nick said, aware that he must have looked a little dishevelled.

The man frowned as he showed their IDs. Nick glanced at them: *Adam Cavendish, Officer, Military Intelligence, Section 5, UK Domestic Counter-intelligence.* The woman, Sophie Greene, had the same ID.

'Is there a problem?' Cavendish asked as he turned off the engine.

'You could say that. We have an unknown number of men inside the safe house. I assume they're here for Abu Habib,' Nick explained.

'Jesus! How the hell did they get in?' Greene said as she took off her seatbelt.

'Through air vents in the garage and up onto the roof. From there, I don't know. My DI was knocked unconscious. There is also a constable still in there somewhere.'

'Do they have firearms?' Cavendish asked, shocked by what Nick was telling him. He and Greene both got out of the car.

'I don't know. I've managed to apprehend one of them. He's tied and gagged over there,' Nick said, pointing into the forest. 'He only had a knife.'

'Okay, thank you, Nick. We need tactical armed support,' Cavendish said, thinking aloud.

Nick liked the sound of that.

'How long will that take?' Nick said.

Greene stared at her phone. 'No signal here?' She sounded anxious.

'Nope. And they've cut the landline and Wi-Fi so we're stuck,' Nick explained.

'Abu Habib is in a holding cell, though?' Cavendish asked.

'Yes. As far as I know,' Nick said.

'Who has the security code for that?' Greene asked.

'DI Hunter,' Nick said.

'Without explosives, there's no way of getting him out of there,' Cavendish said.

'Unless they get the code from DI Hunter,' Greene said with a grim expression.

Nick was all too aware of that uncomfortable thought.

Cavendish looked purposeful. 'Okay, the last time we had a 4G signal was on the main road. Sophie, drive back to the main road and make a call for back-up. We're going to need a Special Forces firearms team here asap.' Cavendish turned to Nick. 'How far is Hereford from here, Nick?'

'About fifty or sixty miles,' Nick said.

Cavendish nodded. 'Sophie, suggest that they chopper up the SAS Counter Terrorist unit. They're close by.'

There was a metallic clunk and then a whirring. At first, Nick couldn't work out what the noise was coming from, or where. Then he realised that the buzzing was the automatic gates across the driveway slowly opening. Nick looked behind him with dread.

'The gates,' Nick said, gesturing and backing away. They had no idea what or who was behind them.

Crack! Crack! Crack! Crack! Crack!

The deafening sound of a machine gun firing replaced the hum of the gates as they opened.

They had no time to react.

Nick dived for the floor and crawled behind the car.

Greene took the full force of the burst of gunfire. Nick could see that she had been hit two or three times in the chest.

'Jesus! Get down!' Nick yelled, instinctively ducking again.

Crack! Crack! Crack! Crack!

The windscreen and headlights of the BMW splintered. The bullets thudded noisily into the car's bodywork and the tyres burst.

Nick watched Cavendish crawl to where Greene had fallen. Maybe he was going to try to pull her to safety. Nick could see there was no point. She was dead.

Nick peered from behind the BMW as the electronic gates continued to open. A man scuttled from behind the large stone pillar and fired an AK-47 from his hip – *Crack! Crack! Crack!*

Nick ducked again as he heard a bullet whizz directly over his head. It thwacked into a tree behind him.

Shit! That was close. This was not good. They were pinned down.

Cavendish crawled around to the back of the car. He looked at Nick as they cowered there.

'Have you got firearms?' Cavendish asked.

'Two Glocks. But they're locked in the armoury in the car. And my DI has the key,' Nick explained. 'You?'

Cavendish shook his head. 'No. This was meant to be routine.'

Crack! Crack! Crack! Crack!

They both flinched again as bullets and glass flew in all directions.

Nick knew that if they stayed there any longer, the man with the AK-47 would assume they were unarmed. He could come out and pick them off like sitting ducks.

'Any ideas?' Cavendish asked.

Then Nick remembered the fireworks he had grabbed from the garage and shoved in his pocket.

'Do you smoke?' Nick asked him.

'What?' Cavendish asked with a furrowed brow.

'I need a lighter,' Nick said as he brought out the Jumping Jack fireworks.

Cavendish gave him a quizzical look, but reached into his jacket pocket, pulled out a lighter and handed it to Nick.

'Cheers,' Nick said, looking down at the bundle of fireworks that were secured together with green string. A white fuse hung out of one end.

Peering around the wing of the car, Nick could see it was about forty yards to the wall where the gates were open. The armed man was still hiding behind the stone pillar.

Clicking the lighter, Nick lit the fuse and watched it fizz and burn.

Throwing the fireworks high into the air, he watched them loop and land at the foot of the wall.

For a few seconds there was nothing. No noise. They hadn't worked. They were pretty old, and maybe they were damp from the garage – or the fuse had gone out.

Suddenly, a loud explosive *bang* boomed out of the darkness. Then another *bang!* And another.

It was exactly what Nick had hoped for. The Jumping Jacks sounded like gunfire.

There was anxious shouting from behind the gates. Then movement as the fireworks continued to explode noisily.

Then Nick heard the metallic clunk and whirr he had heard earlier. The gates creaked and then slowly closed.

Bingo! At least they think we're armed now, Nick thought as he shared a look with Cavendish.

'I thought I'd seen everything,' Cavendish said.

'Yeah, well I used to be a big fan of *The A-Team*,' Nick quipped as the gates closed with a clang.

CHAPTER 13

5.50 pm

THE SOUND OF GUNFIRE outside was making Ruth unbearably anxious. She had no idea what was going on or what had happened. Nick was out there – was he still alive? Had Hamzar gone out and shot the two MI5 agents dead? Were the MI5 agents armed? The pit of her stomach was tight and she felt like she was going to be sick.

Ruth shifted on her chair – the plastic zip ties were permanently digging into the skin on her wrists. She was coming to the slow realisation that the only way out of this would be getting help from outside. But no one knew they were in trouble. Had the MI5 agents managed to contact someone to tell them what had happened?

Glancing over at Sameer, she could see he was transfixed by the bank of CCTV monitors. He was jigging one of his legs, again and again, his moves quick and jittery. With every burst of gunfire, he flinched.

He leant down and hit a button on the keyboard. Outside fell silent. Ruth could only partially see one monitor from where she was sitting. What was going on? Was Nick dead? Had the MI5 agents stopped the attackers? She squinted to get a better angle; it was an overview of the whole front area of the house. The picture was hard to make out in the night vision, but she could see the slow progression of the gates, which were closing. The button Sameer clicked must have closed the gates. But why?

'What's going on?' Ruth asked. 'Why have you closed the gates?'

Sameer ignored her and rubbed his face and nose.

'You don't have to do this, Sameer. You know that?' Ruth said in a gentle tone.

'Shut up,' Sameer growled.

Sameer looked over at her. Was there a way of getting to him before the others got back?

'Sameer, you seem to be a reasonable and intelligent man. My guess is that you got involved in this because you thought it was a simple rescue mission. You would get here, break Abu Habib from his cell, and leave. But it's not turning out like that, is it? It's a mess and you're in the middle of it,' Ruth said, hoping she'd got the right measure of the man.

Sameer got up and glared at her. Ruth held her breath. Was he going to come over and hit her?

'I know what you're trying to do and I'm not interested in what someone like you has to say,' Sameer said as he went back to staring at the monitors.

'You're running out of options, Sameer. Yasir has disappeared. The people who arrived were agents for MI5. If anything happens to them, or if they make contact with the outside, then you've got about half an hour before a unit of heavily armed officers scale the walls. And they won't be arresting you. They will shoot you on sight,' Ruth said.

Sameer snapped to his feet and came over. 'I've already told you to shut up!' he yelled in her face.

He doesn't have it in him to hit me, Ruth thought. Prayed.

'Sorry, Sameer. But you need to do the right thing and let me go before Hamzar gets back. You can see what kind of man he is. He will go down fighting, and you'll get killed alongside him. And that's not what you thought was going to happen tonight, is it?' Ruth said in a stronger tone.

From the corner of her left eye, Ruth saw a figure move outside in the hallway and then disappear again. At first, she assumed it was Hamzar and Kashif returning from outside. Then she realised it was PC Garrow.

Sameer didn't appear to be armed. However, the bag that Hamzar had taken the AK-47 from clearly had other weapons inside it. If PC Garrow came in, would Sameer get to the bag in time? Did Sameer even have it in him to shoot someone? She didn't want to find out.

Sameer paced the room. He looked at the monitors again. His breathing was quick and shallow – he was panicking. Maybe what she had said to him was making him question what he was doing there. Maybe he was terrified that an SAS unit would arrive and shoot them all dead.

Glancing left, Ruth saw a shadow being thrown across the carpet by the doorway. PC Garrow was outside. Sameer was pacing back and could turn to face the door at any moment. She couldn't let him see Garrow. Ruth wracked her brain for something to say. It was only a matter of time before Sameer would catch sight of the shadow.

'Do you have family, Sameer?' Ruth asked. The man stopped and leant on the table underneath the bank of monitors, his fingers drumming on the surface nervously. 'Do they know you're here? Do they know what you're doing?'

Sameer shook his head as he moved across the room again.

'Maybe you should call them, check how they are? If it all goes wrong, this might be your last chance to speak to them,' Ruth suggested.

'I'm not falling for that so easily. My family will understand why I'm doing this. Plus, I'm not stupid. I'm not going to leave you here on your own,' Sameer said with a sneer.

'I'm not going anywhere, Sameer,' Ruth said, gesturing with her head to her bound hands. 'To think, you'll never hear their voices again.'

Sameer's expression faltered for a moment. He stopped pacing and held his head in his hands. Ruth's plan had worked. Sameer pulled a phone from his pocket and held it, staring at it for a moment. 'Stay there!' he growled at her and moved towards the doorway.

'Sameer!' Ruth said loudly to distract him. 'Sameer!'

Sameer was startled and turned to look at her. 'What?'

In that split second, PC Garrow thundered through the doorway. He launched himself at Sameer and bundled him to the floor. Ruth could see that PC Garrow was carrying a large knife that he must have taken from the kitchen.

The two men wrestled, but the young constable was clearly far stronger. He pinned Sameer to the ground.

'Help me!' Sameer yelled in a slightly pitiful tone.

Ruth felt helpless – she needed PC Garrow to cut the zip ties.

PC Garrow punched Sameer hard in the face and then reached for the handcuffs that he carried on his belt. But Sameer pushed him off balance. PC Garrow dropped the knife as he tumbled to one side.

Sameer scrambled to his feet, his eyes wide with fear.

'Don't let him get to that bag!' Ruth yelled, but it was too late.

Searching inside the bag, Sameer pulled out a huge machete and waved it at PC Garrow, who was now unarmed – he was only two yards away. Sameer's hand trembled uncontrollably.

'Put that down,' PC Garrow said.

'Sameer, you're not going to kill someone in cold blood. I know you're not that kind of man,' Ruth said.

'You know nothing about me!' Sameer was getting hysterical. He puffed out his cheeks as he tried to get his breath.

PC Garrow took a cautious step forward. 'Come on.'

'Jim,' Ruth said, sounding a note of caution.

'Stay back!' Sameer yelled. 'I'll cut you.' The machete was shaking dangerously in his hand.

PC Garrow took another step forward and held out his hand to take the machete.

Suddenly, Ruth saw Sameer raise the machete into the air.

He's going to attack him!

'Jim!' Ruth shouted.

PC Garrow took a step backwards. Sameer swung the machete at his head, but he ducked and lunged forward. He tried to put Sameer in a neck lock. Sameer elbowed him in the throat. They wrestled and crashed over the table. They rolled on top of the table until Sameer made a move for PC Garrow. He held the machete to the young constable's neck. Ruth couldn't bear to watch as the silver blade quivered at her colleague's throat.

But, in one swift movement, PC Garrow spun out of Sameer's grip, grabbed the kitchen knife from the floor, plunged it into Sameer's chest, and pulled it out.

Lying back on the floor, Sameer was gasping for breath. He coughed blood into the air.

A second later, PC Garrow was cutting the plastic ties from Ruth's wrists. There was no time to lose.

'Are you all right, ma'am?' he asked.

'Am *I* all right? You nearly had your head cut off,' Ruth said, rubbing her wrists, trying to get rid of the pain.

'Come on,' PC Garrow said, as they dashed out of the surveillance room and into the large hallway.

Ruth gestured to the front door. 'This way.'

'I'm not sure that's a good idea,' PC Garrow said under his breath.

Ruth had thoughts of somehow getting out to the car and retrieving the Glocks from the locked armoury. Going out the front was dangerous, but having the guns might be the only way for them to stand a chance of leaving this place alive.

PC Garrow held back as Ruth moved swiftly to the front door that had been left open by about a foot. Ducking her head to look out, Ruth saw Hamzar and Kashif jogging up the steps and arguing. Just as she was about to reel her head in, the two men looked up. *Shit.*

Hamzar had spotted Ruth. He pulled a sadistic grin and brought his weapon up to face her. He opened fire.

Crack! Crack! Crack!

Bullets ricocheted off the door frame as Ruth leapt back.

They sprinted back into the hallway. Glancing behind for a second, Ruth then looked at the enormous staircase leading to the first floor. There was a maze of rooms upstairs, which might buy them some time.

'Upstairs,' Ruth said. She could hear the shouts of Hamzar and Kashif approaching.

Ruth and PC Garrow leapt up the steps, fully expecting to hear a cacophony of gunfire behind them any second. Knowing that they would be easy targets on the staircase, Ruth also half expected to feel a bullet in her back.

With her heart hammering, Ruth reached the top. She spun around. PC Garrow was just behind her.

'Keep going, ma'am,' PC Garrow gasped.

They darted along the central corridor on the first floor. Then they turned left, passing various closed doors.

Up ahead was the security door to the holding cell where Abu Habib was being kept.

'Go in there, ma'am,' PC Garrow said urgently, pointing to the door.

'What?' Ruth said.

'No one else has the code. They can't get in,' he said, virtually pushing Ruth towards the cell. He had a good point. They would be safe in there – at least in the short term.

'Wait, where the hell are you going?' Ruth said, frantically glancing back down the corridor. Hamzar and Kashif wouldn't be far behind.

'Don't worry about me, ma'am,' he said with surprising confidence.

Jesus, he's got some balls, Ruth thought.

She grabbed her keys and pushed them into his palm.

'In the car, on the passenger-side footwell. There's an armoury with two handguns,' Ruth said, rushing to get out her words.

As Ruth looked at the keypad, PC Garrow zipped back down the corridor, through a doorway and out of sight.

Punching in the code, she went to open the door. Nothing. It was the wrong one. *For fuck's sake, Ruth. Remember the code!*

She heard shouting. They were getting closer.

Ruth tried again. Nothing.

Her head was whirling. *Jesus! What was it? Quickly!*

She tried again.

Clunk!

The locks of the door opened. She pushed down the handle and threw herself inside. The door closed and automatically locked behind her.

Abu Habib was sitting up on the bed. He seemed calm. Ruth knew that he would have heard the gunshots from outside. Surely, he would wonder what the hell was going on? Unless he already knew it was going to happen.

Lurching across the room, Ruth dived to the floor and squeezed herself close to the wall. From here, she couldn't be seen from the viewing window.

However, Abu could easily indicate to someone at the door that Ruth was inside. But whatever happened, Hamzar and Kashif couldn't get in. The door was made from reinforced steel.

Gasping for breath, Ruth sat against the wall.

'What's going on?' Abu asked in a measured voice.

Ruth looked at him. What was she going to tell him?

'Looks like your friends are here to rescue you,' Ruth said.

'You think they are my friends?' Abu said, shaking his head.

Suddenly, there was banging at the door. She could hear Hamzar shouting and hitting the glass of the observation window. Maybe he was trying to use the butt of the AK-47 to smash his way through. He wouldn't get very far.

Abu looked up at the window. His face was virtually expressionless.

Why isn't he telling them that I'm in here?

There was more shouting and banging from outside.

Abu looked back from the door and settled himself on the bed, picking up his book.

What the hell is he doing? Has the man lost it? Why is he covering for me?

After a few seconds, the noise from outside stopped. Hamzar and Kashif had given up trying to get in – for the meantime.

'I don't understand,' Ruth said, with her pulse still racing.

'What don't you understand?' Abu said in a gentle voice.

'Why didn't you tell them I was in here? Why did you cover for me?' Ruth asked.

'I told you these men are not my friends,' Abu said.

'But they're here to rescue you, aren't they?' Ruth said – but then the penny dropped.

'No. I'm afraid they're here to kill me.'

CHAPTER 14

6.08 pm

THE SHOOTING HAD STOPPED, but Nick and Cavendish remained crouched behind the car, waiting until they were sure it was safe. Nick could still feel his pulse drumming Keith Moon-style in his ears.

'What do you think?' Cavendish asked.

Nick nodded. 'I don't think they're coming back.' He wasn't a hundred per cent sure, but they couldn't hide behind the car all night. He needed to get Ruth to safety.

Standing gingerly, the muscles in Nick's legs ached from crouching. His broken toes now throbbed rhythmically in sync with his pulse.

'Come on. I'll show you how we get back over,' Nick said.

As they moved stealthily towards the wall in the darkness, Nick's mind spun with what had just happened. How were they going to get Ruth out of the house? The fact that the men had an AK-47 had just upped the stakes. How would they get away? Would he get back to see Amanda? What he would give to be transported back to Llancastell safely. Everything. Anything. What if he never saw her again? What if his child grew up without a father? Nick was struck by a physical pain in his heart at the agonising possibility that he might never get to meet his baby.

All was quiet and still. The only noise now was from himself and Cavendish as they negotiated the trees by moonlight.

Suddenly, there was movement in the leaves up ahead. A banging noise. Nick froze and held his breath.

He and Cavendish exchanged a look.

As the dry leaves were thrown up into the air, two large wood pigeons flapped noisily and flew up and away into the trees above them.

Jesus Christ!

Nick looked at Cavendish and gestured to his torch as if to ask, 'Is it all right to use it here?' Cavendish nodded.

Worried that they might be spotted coming into the compound at the point that Nick had made his escape, they retrieved the tarpaulin – the material thick enough that the razor wire didn't cause any tears as they pulled it down to them. Clicking on the LED torch, they walked in silence along the wall, looking for a way over – they needed to get back into the compound. Nick wasn't going to leave two police officers held hostage – especially not Ruth.

'This looks good.' Cavendish pointed to a tree up ahead that had grown close to the wall.

Nick agreed. If they could get onto the higher branches, they could literally jump down onto the top of the wall. They could lower the tarpaulin down first to cover the razor wire.

'I'll go first,' Cavendish said, full of confidence.

Nick wasn't going to argue – he felt exhausted and battered. It was an effort to keep walking, let alone start climbing trees.

Cupping his hands to offer Cavendish a boost, Nick looked at him. 'Here you go.'

Cavendish waved his hand as he went to the tree. 'It's all right. Climbing's my thing.'

Pulling the tarpaulin with him, Cavendish went up the first few branches like they were shallow stairs. His upper-body strength was impressive.

Climbing really is his thing! Nick thought.

Nick noticed the silence of the night air. He looked up at the moon that was partially covered by clouds. The moon with its blood-smeared face. Nick didn't believe in omens. Right now, he couldn't let his mind entertain it. He had to concentrate, but he couldn't shake the sense of foreboding as its ominous red-stained light hung over them like a noose.

'Your turn,' Cavendish called down quietly, breaking Nick's train of thought.

Following the path that Cavendish had taken up the branches, Nick used every ounce of strength he had left to get to the huge branch that Cavendish was sitting astride. As he pushed down with his foot, the searing pain from his broken toes was unbearable.

'Jesus!' Nick hissed through his teeth as he screwed up his face in pain.

'Okay?' Cavendish asked. He pulled Nick up the last few feet.

'Never better.'

'Don't suppose this is what you had planned for this evening?'

'I'm meant to be in Llancastell at the birth of my first child,' Nick said.

Cavendish shook his head. 'You're kidding?'

'I wish I was.'

Cavendish looked directly at Nick. 'Don't worry. We'll get you back to see your baby. I promise you that.'

Something about the utter confidence with which Cavendish spoke to him gave Nick the boost he needed. He was going to get Ruth out of there. And then he would get back home to see the love of his life and their child. And fuck anyone who got in his way.

Having lowered the canvas over the razor wire, Nick and Cavendish dropped onto the wall top. As Nick looked down the other side, he nearly lost his balance. He squatted down and grabbed on to the thick canvas to brace himself, inches from where the glinting metal of the razor wire had cut through the tarpaulin.

Edging himself over the side, Nick took his bodyweight on his bent arms. As he tried to lower himself, he felt his muscles begin to shake. His body had had enough. He was completely drained and didn't know how much – if anything – he had left in the tank. He clambered down and then stood with his weight on his heels to stop the pain in his toes.

'Where's the terrorist that you captured?' Cavendish asked.

Nick pointed to a spot in the wooded area further inside the compound. 'Just over there.'

'Let's see if he can tell us anything useful,' Cavendish said, and they began to weave through the trees and undergrowth.

Nick was anxious. He didn't really care about what was going on with the attackers – he just wanted Ruth out of the safe house and the hell out of there. This was MI5's hole to deal with. 'Look, they've got my DI. The longer she's in there, the more harm she can come to.'

'I agree. And I understand your sense of urgency, but the more information we have, the better prepared we are. And the more likely it is that we can get her out of there safely,' Cavendish said.

Nick nodded. He knew Cavendish was making a cogent point.

For a few minutes, they walked in silence, pushing branches away and moving in and out of the trees.

'Had you worked with Officer Greene for long?' Nick asked. He couldn't help seeing the image in his mind of her dead body just lying there beside the car.

'Sophie? A few weeks. She's just moved over from a stint in Ireland ...' Cavendish said, catching himself using the present tense. 'Or, she had ...'

Nick didn't know what to say next and concluded that not saying anything was the best policy. They walked in silence again. The only sound was the swish of branches and the twigs and leaves under their feet.

As they reached the small clearing, Nick flashed the torch over to the man who was still tied to the tree with a gag in his mouth. He squinted at the torchlight in his eyes. The eye socket was purple and puffy where Nick had kicked him.

'If you want, I can handle this,' Cavendish said, gesturing to the man. 'I worked in interrogation in Kabul for a while.'

'Help yourself,' Nick said.

Taking the light, Cavendish crouched down in front of him. 'I'm going to take this gag out of your mouth. And I'm going to ask you some questions, which you are going to answer. If you shout for help, then I am going to cause you a serious

amount of pain and damage. Do you understand what I said?'
Cavendish said.

Cavendish's calm, cold demeanour and voice made Nick
feel a little uneasy. There was a crackle from the man's clothing.
Cavendish went into a side pocket, pulled out a walkie-talkie
and handed it to Nick. The airwaves were silent, but it didn't
mean that his accomplices hadn't clocked he was missing.

Removing the gag, Cavendish looked at the man for a second. 'What's your name?'

The man looked at him and glared.

Cavendish threw a punch straight into the man's nose,
splitting it.

Jesus Christ. He's not messing about! Nick thought, a little
shocked.

'Try that again. What's your name?' Cavendish said calmly.
After a second or two of silence, Cavendish feigned a punch.

'Yasir,' the man mumbled.

'Yasir? Right, good,' Cavendish said in a tone that was almost too polite.

Yasir looked terrified. Something about Cavendish had
spooked him.

'Good. I want you to tell me how many of you there are
here?' Cavendish asked.

Yasir shook his head and said nothing.

'Oh dear, this isn't a good start,' Cavendish said. In a flash,
he had reached out, grabbed Yasir's nose, which forced him
to open his mouth. He pushed the gag roughly back into his
mouth. He reached around, grabbed his hand and snapped his
middle finger in half. It sounded like a twig breaking. He then
snapped another finger.'

Even through the gag, Nick could hear Yasir scream. It was a horrendous noise. Nick tried not to flinch. The spooks did things a little differently to North Wales Police.

'Okay. If you don't tell me what I need to know, I'm going to break the rest of your fingers one by one,' Cavendish said.

Reaching over, he pulled the gag out. 'How many, Yasir?'

Yasir had tears in his eyes from the pain, but he shook his head.

As Cavendish reached for the gag again, Yasir sat upright. 'Four. There are four of us.'

'Good. That wasn't so hard,' Cavendish said. 'Weapons. You have an AK-47. Are there any other weapons?'

'A gun. A revolver. That is all, I promise,' Yasir said, shaking.

'Now, are you here tonight to rescue Abu Habib? Is that right?'

Yasir thought about the question and frowned. 'Yes ... umm, that's right ...'

CHAPTER 15

RUTH AND ABU HAD HARDLY exchanged any words since her abrupt arrival. Even though she knew that the door was made from reinforced steel and glass, she had no idea how much force it could withstand. She was fairly certain that if the men got through the door, they would shoot both her and Abu dead with little hesitation.

Her mind turned to Ella. *What is she doing right now?* Ruth wondered. She felt guilty that she had put her daughter through so much emotional turmoil over the years. Sometimes she was astonished by Ella's maturity and resilience. An old head on young shoulders. Was yesterday going to be the last time she would ever see her daughter? She had nearly lost her the Christmas before last. With a gritty resolve, Ruth wasn't about to leave Ella motherless. She was going to get out of this bloody place alive!

'You can take these off, you know?' Abu said, gesturing to the handcuffs that secured him to the bed.

'I don't have the key,' Ruth said. She wasn't lying. PC Garrow had the key and she hadn't thought to take it.

But if I did, I wouldn't be unlocking your cuffs.

Where was PC Garrow? The lack of noise or gunfire was a good sign. Unless they had already got to him ... She prayed that he was somewhere safe and unharmed. If he could get to the armoury in the car, then she might get out of this nightmare intact. It would be even better if PC Garrow could contact Nick – that was if Nick was still alive.

Nick was meant to be travelling back home at this precise moment to be with his pregnant fiancée. Instead, he was dodging terrorist bullets – or worse. It made her angry that they had been given the task of taking Abu Habib. The idea that it was just a bit of babysitting was a bloody joke. They should have sent Armed Response with them, not left them hanging out to dry.

'If you unlock my handcuffs, I won't harm you,' Abu said as he took off his glasses and wiped them.

'You would blow innocent women and children to pieces, but you wouldn't harm me,' Ruth said in a withering tone. 'How does that work?'

Ruth wasn't going to put up with Abu's bullshit.

'You think I'm a murdering, evil monster?' Abu asked.

'You know what? I'm not interested in you or what you stand for. If you think it's okay to kill innocent civilians, then that makes you inhuman,' Ruth snapped.

'Killing innocent civilians is inhuman then?' Abu asked.

'Yes, of course!' Ruth said. 'How can it not be?'

'Do you know how many thousands of innocent civilians have been killed in Afghanistan, Iraq or Syria by drone attacks or allied bombings?' Abu said.

'That's different. That's a war zone,' Ruth replied, although she was annoyed that she had been drawn into an argument and that her words were being used against her.

'Oh, it is their fault they died because they happen to live in a war zone?' Abu asked with a condescending smirk. 'And you say that I am inhuman ... Let me ask you something.'

Ruth inwardly groaned – she wished she hadn't said anything now.

'A young British soldier dies in Afghanistan. On the news you see his parents, his coffin being flown home. It does not matter that he died five thousand miles away. You still feel sad, and you still feel angry. It is the same,' Abu said calmly.

Ruth gestured to the door. 'And yet, you have men out there waiting to kill you. How does that fit into your theory of a united Muslim brotherhood?'

'Those men have been fed lies and misinformation by the secret services of your government. They now believe that I am a traitor. That I will tell MI5 and Special Branch where the ISIS terrorist cells are in Britain. Or at least the ones I know of. Our communication links to Afghanistan. Training camps. Everything,' Abu said.

'But you're not? You're not a traitor then?' Ruth asked.

'No, far from it,' Abu said. 'I am no kind of traitor.'

The conversation died for a few seconds.

Ruth was trying to work out her next move. She could sit tight and hope that the MI5 agents that had arrived had managed to call for back-up. Failing that, Nick and PC Garrow were out there somewhere.

Ruth looked at him. 'What?'

'Your accent. You sound like you're from London,' Abu said.

'Look, I know we're stuck in this room together, but we're really not going to do the whole "getting to know you" routine.

You're a terrorist. And I'm a police officer,' Ruth said. She just wanted to sit quietly so that she could go through all the options that were available to her.

'You've clearly read my file. And I guess you think you know all about me?' Abu said.

'All I need to know, thank you,' Ruth growled at him across the room.

'So what's your next move? You can't sit here for ev—'

Bang! Bang! Bang!

There were three booming metallic thuds against the door.

The men were back. It sounded like they had some kind of sledgehammer with them. Ruth was sure that they couldn't get through the door with just that.

'Here they come,' Abu said dryly.

'You don't seem particularly worried,' Ruth said.

'"Every soul shall taste death, and only on the Day of Judgement will you be paid your full recompense." To face death with that kind of certainty is a gift from Allah,' Abu said. 'I'm ready.'

Ruth ignored him. She could hear another sound from outside. A whirring, low drone that seemed to get louder. Then a deafening, grating metallic sound.

Bloody hell! They've got a drill, Ruth thought in a panic.

The drilling stopped momentarily. Abu looked over at her. 'If they have the right drill bits, then that door will be open in the next ten minutes.'

Ruth knew he was right. An industrial drill could pierce the metal and destroy the locks.

'Are *you* ready, officer?' Abu asked.

'What?' Ruth snapped at him angrily.

'Are you ready to meet your God?'
The drilling started again.

CHAPTER 16

6.42 pm

NICK AND CAVENDISH had got little more out of Yasir except for that there were four men, they had an AK-47 and a handgun, and they that had come to rescue Abu Habib. Having gagged Yasir again, they had brought him with them – Cavendish thought they could trade. Hand over Ruth and PC Garrow in return for Yasir. Nick was willing to try anything to rescue Ruth.

Nick had felt uncomfortable watching Cavendish's brutal but cold 'interrogation'. However, it did also occur to him that sometimes when he was sitting in the room with a paedophile or a rapist, he would have gladly broken their fingers one by one. For a second, he thought of Curtis Blake, the infamous Liverpudlian drug dealer and gangster. Nick had been trying to get his revenge on Blake for years. Nick still blamed him for his girlfriend Laura's death back in 2003. Even though Blake was now serving a relatively brief prison sentence, Nick would like to have dished out some of the spook's techniques on him.

Cavendish had found a series of documents alongside a hunting knife that had been hidden in a secret pocket in Yasir's clothing. As they approached the edge of the woods, Cavendish unfolded the documents. He spread them out on the trunk of a fallen tree.

135

'Let's see what we've got,' Cavendish said, using the torch as he flicked through the papers.

Nick was frustrated with all these delays. He knew they needed to have as much information as possible, but he also needed Ruth out of that house safely, and soon. The longer she was being held captive in there, the more danger she was in. The documents could contain something useful, or they could just be Yasir's weekly shopping list!

As Cavendish worked through the papers at an eye-wateringly slow pace, Nick spotted something that looked like a list of times, names and places. Underneath that was a detailed map of what must have been the safe house and surrounding area. A red cross marked a point on the perimeter wall over on the west side, opposite to where they were now. The word *van* had been scrawled next to the cross.

'This is where they parked and came over the wall,' Nick said to Cavendish, pointing to the X on the map.

'I assume the plan was to break Habib out, get over the wall here, and away in the van. Any other modes of transport?' Cavendish said, thinking out loud.

'The BMW you arrived in is out of action with a hundred bullets in it. They slashed the tyres on our Astra. So, I guess not,' Nick said.

'Did you find any keys on Yasir?' Cavendish asked.

Nick could see that Yasir had been mentally broken, along with his fingers, by the interrogation. He shuffled with the odd groan of pain.

Nick shook his head. 'No. Nothing. Someone else inside must have them.'

A few minutes later, they walked out of the edge of the forest, and into the shadowy compound of the safe house.

'Let's see if we can trade,' Nick said as he took the walkie-talkie and looked at Cavendish. Nick pressed the black rubber button to open the channel. 'This is Detective Sergeant Nick Evans. We have Yasir here with us. Meet us outside.'

Cavendish took the knife that they had found on Yasir, pulled him in front of him and held the blade to his throat. As far as the other terrorists knew, Cavendish and Nick had a firearm, which gave them more bargaining power.

Every second they waited for a response was agony. Who was to know whether the intruders were still in the house? Had they got to Ruth already and driven off with their special guest in tow? Nick's nerves were frayed. His body ached all over, and the adrenaline had made him a little shaky. Taking his sleeve, he wiped sweat from his forehead.

The security door at the front of the safe house opened very slowly. A corridor of light fell over the gravel. Then two shadowy figures appeared and began to approach, their boots crunching in a slow rhythm on the stones. Nick's eyes adjusted as he tried to take in as much detail as he could. He squinted, but all he could see were shapes. He wiped the salty sweat from his brow and top lip again. His chest heaved as he took a long breath.

A soft whisper of wind picked up a small pile of leaves and scattered them noisily across the gravel. Then another mound of leaves skittered back the other way.

Bloody hell! Come on!

The slow pace was frustrating him. The tension in his stomach tightened. How was this going to go? Were they going to do a trade? Nick took another deep breath and tried to release it slowly. The nerves in his whole body seemed to jangle as they waited. His fingers patted and danced against his side.

Come on! Come on! What are we waiting for?

The two men moved out of the shadow of the door and into the light of the supermoon and stopped. Like the Mexican stand-off scene in a dubbed spaghetti western, no one said anything for a few seconds.

The taller, skinnier of the two was young. He blinked. A lot. It was clear he was very nervous. He wore a black kufi and had an AK-47 slung over his shoulder. The shorter, thick-set man seemed calm as he moved again, out of the shadows and into the light.

'Here we go,' Cavendish muttered under his breath.

'That's far enough,' Nick shouted when they were about forty yards away. His heart was banging in his chest. He had to get this right if he was going to save Ruth's life.

No one said anything.

'What do you want?' the thick-set man sneered. His accent had a French-African lilt to it.

'You have two of our officers inside. We want them out here safely,' Nick said.

The younger man gave the other a look of slight confusion – Nick picked up on it. He knew they had Ruth – he had seen her knocked unconscious and taken. Maybe they didn't have PC Garrow. They might not even know he's in there. Now they were in a complicated game of bluff.

'Yes. And you give us Yasir? Is that what you are suggesting?' the thick-set man asked.

'Exactly,' Nick said.

At least we agree, Nick thought, with a tiny glimmer of hope.

'What about Abu Habib?' the man said.

'My guess is that you don't have the code,' Nick said.

Why else would they still be in the house?

'Maybe. Either way, we will be in that room and have Abu Habib in about ten minutes. Then we will have what we came for,' the man said.

Nick didn't know what he meant. The inference was that with or without the code, they would get into the holding cell and release Abu Habib. He wasn't sure how they would do that unless they had specialist equipment or explosives. However, either way, Nick was sure they would not leave without Yasir.

Nick gestured to Yasir. 'You won't have everything, will you? ... Simple trade. You bring our officers out here unharmed, then we'll let you have Yasir. Whether or not you take Abu Habib with you isn't my concern.'

Come on, come on. Let's get this done so we can all get out of here alive, Nick thought.

'I've already lost a colleague tonight. We don't want anyone else to die. Just bring the officers out here,' Cavendish said with a calm confidence.

The thick-set man took a few steps forward, which unnerved Nick.

'Stay where you are!' Nick barked.

What the fuck is he doing?

The man put up his hands and then opened his robe. 'Don't worry. I am not armed ... What if we refuse? You're not going to kill Yasir, are you?'

'I won't, no. But I'm afraid my friend here works for MI5. And they're a law unto themselves,' Nick said.

There were a few more seconds of tense silence. Cavendish stood motionless, his eyes locked on those of the man in front of them.

Nick had given up on God a long time ago, but in those moments where everything was teetering on a knife edge, he pleaded with any higher power that would listen to allow Ruth out of there safely.

'If you don't want to take Yasir, then we can hand him over to our interrogators and to the CIA. I'm sure they'll persuade Yasir to tell us all about your group, your activities, plans,' Cavendish said. 'After all, that's why you came for Abu Habib tonight, isn't it? You didn't want him to fall into the hands of the Security Service, did you?'

The man considered what Cavendish had said and then exchanged a look with the younger man. He shrugged.

'I don't see that you have any other choice,' Cavendish said.

The thick-set man looked at the floor and then nodded.

Nick breathed a sigh of relief – *Thank you, God. I owe you one.*

'Well, we do have another choice,' the man muttered half to himself.

Suddenly, the thick-set man reached behind inside his robe. As if in slow motion, he pulled a handgun from the waistband of his trousers.

Nick dived for the floor instinctively. He watched the man raise the gun to Yasir's chest. *Crack! Crack! Crack!*

'*No!*' Nick yelled, turning to see both Cavendish and Yasir falling to the ground.

Scrambling to his feet, Nick looked to his right. Yasir had three dark bullet holes in his torso – he was dead.

Nick grabbed Cavendish and pulled him from the ground. *Crack! Crack!*

Two more gunshots exploded as they sprinted for the cover of the trees.

CHAPTER 17

6.41 pm

THE DRILLING HAD LASTED for about ten minutes before it suddenly stopped. Ruth prayed that it was because the men trying to drill their way through the door had given up. Maybe they just weren't able to get through the door? The other, more sickening possibility was they were almost through and were just preparing themselves for battle ...

What's my next move? Ruth wondered. While she was in the holding cell, she was safe. And no one could assassinate Abu Habib while the door still held. However, whilst she was 'safe' inside, God knows what PC Garrow and Nick were doing out there. If they were still alive.

The silence that haunted them as they awaited their fate was suddenly broken by gunfire. Two or three shots. It wasn't the sound of the AK-47 – Ruth could tell that immediately. More like a handgun. Had PC Garrow managed to get the guns from the car armoury?

Jesus! This is so frustrating, not knowing what's going on out there.

Ruth glanced over at Abu, who was sitting with his eyes closed, despite the gunfire. How was he remaining so calm? There were terrorists who wanted to kill him trying to break down the door.

Ruth crawled over to a small sink in the corner of the room. Above that was a tiny square mirror attached to the wall. Taking off her shoe, Ruth crouched in front of the basin. She glanced back at the window on the security door. Nothing.

Reaching up, and with all her strength, Ruth smashed the heel of her shoe into the mirror. It cracked a little – but not as much as she wanted.

'What are you doing?' Abu asked. She ignored him.

Hitting the mirror again, three pieces of it broke away and fell down into the sink.

'Seven years bad luck, that.' Abu smiled.

There is something seriously wrong with that man.

Taking some nicotine gum from her pocket, she popped it in her mouth and chewed. She then glanced around the room, but she couldn't see anything that would help.

Then she had a thought. Taking one of her earrings out of her ear, she unbent the hoop. When she had finished, she had a straight piece of plated silver that was about three inches long. She took the gum from her mouth and attached it to the top. Taking a shard of mirror, she stuck that to the chewing gum.

Shuffling across the floor, Ruth got to the door. Abu gave her a curious look, as if she had gone mad.

Sitting with her back to the door, Ruth raised the mirror that was now attached to the long earring handle up to the window in the door. She tilted it slightly. From where she was sitting, she could see down the corridor without having to put her face to the window. The corridor was empty – wherever the men had gone, they weren't back yet.

'Neat trick,' Abu said.

'I saw it on a film once. Clint Eastwood, I think,' Ruth said.

'*Escape from Alcatraz*,' Abu said.

'Probably,' Ruth said under her breath as she tried to work out what to do next.

'What's the plan?' Abu asked with more than a hint of sarcasm.

'As far as I see it, you need me to stay alive,' Ruth said.

'Do I?' Abu said. 'I was preparing to blow myself to pieces yesterday. Why would dying here bother me?'

Ruth looked at him. 'Because blowing yourself, and dozens of others, to smithereens in the middle of Manchester strikes a powerful blow in the course of your holy jihad. You believe you will be rewarded in heaven for your courage and sacrifice. Am I right?'

Abu shrugged. 'Go on.'

'Being found dead in a ditch in North Wales with a bullet in your head doesn't really further the cause of a united Islam, does it? And you take the risk of not being received as a brave jihadist hero when you arrive in heaven. Not sure Allah's welcome will be quite so hearty,' Ruth said.

'Okay. So what's your plan?' Abu asked, sounding disinterested.

'There's no one out there. And no one knows I'm in here. If I can find PC Garrow, I can get the keys to your cuffs. Then I can get you out of here before we all get killed,' Ruth explained.

'Why not leave me here? You could take your chances without me,' Abu said.

'My job was to bring you here and keep you safe. I can't leave you here to get murdered in cold blood,' Ruth said.

Abu let out an audible sigh as Ruth glanced back at the mirror. The corridor was still clear.

'If that is the case, then there's something you should know,' Abu said.

'What's that?' Ruth asked. She retrieved the mirror and sat up against the door, preparing herself for more of Abu's radical nonsense.

'I'm a police officer,' Abu said.

Ruth was convinced she had misheard him.

'Sorry?' Ruth asked, her brow furrowed.

Abu took a few seconds and then said, 'I am a police officer. My name is Detective Inspector Abu Mallik of the North West Counterterrorism Unit.'

Ruth couldn't believe her ears. *Surely, he can't be telling the truth.*

'What are you talking about?' Ruth said, still trying to get her head around what she had just been told.

'I've been an undercover officer in an Islamic terrorist cell in Manchester for the last three years,' Abu said. 'I have been feeding information back to Special Branch and MI5 about terrorist plots in North West England.'

Ruth ran everything he had said, and what they had been told at the Special Branch briefing, through her mind – there was simply no way that this man could be an undercover police officer.

'This is bollocks! If you're an undercover officer, then why have we brought you to an MI5 safe house?' Ruth asked.

'I'm debriefing officers from MI5 after yesterday's events in Manchester,' Abu replied.

'That makes no sense. You were going to blow yourself up yesterday,' Ruth said as questions whirled around her mind.

'How do you think Counterterrorism knew we were there?' Abu asked.

'What about the man they shot? He was carrying explosives,' Ruth asked.

'Yes. He was part of the terrorist cell. But the rucksack he was wearing, the explosives weren't wired to explode,' Abu explained.

'Nice try. You're very convincing, but I've been a police officer far too long to believe what you're telling me,' Ruth said.

Abu reached down and removed one of his shoes.

What the hell is he doing now?

Twisting the heel, Abu opened a small compartment inside the sole of his boot. It was no bigger than a postage stamp. He tapped it and out fell a small plastic square – it looked like a tiny memory card for a digital camera.

'If I'm not an undercover police officer, then why do I have this tracking device in my shoe?' Abu asked.

Ruth shrugged. 'I don't know.'

'Were you briefed this morning before bringing me here?' Abu asked.

'Yes ...' Ruth replied hesitantly.

'Two officers from Special Branch went through who I was?'

'Yes ...'

'One of whom was Detective Inspector Gary Brunton?' Abu asked.

'Yeah, how do you know that?' Ruth asked with a quizzical look.

Maybe he is telling the truth ...

'DI Brunton is my handler. He recruited me to work as an undercover operative. How would I know any of that if I was an Islamic terrorist working out of Didsbury?' Abu asked.

Ruth looked at him. He had made a very convincing case.

Before she could say anything else, Ruth was startled by a crunching noise. The drilling had started again.

CHAPTER 18

7.04 pm

THE BRUTALITY WITH which Yasir had been killed had thrown Nick. As a police officer and a detective, he usually arrived at a crime scene after the event. He was witness to the results of extreme violence. However, today he had seen two people shot dead, and it was hard to process. Watching the life drain from a person who had been alive right in front of you only moments before was something he would never get used to.

What worried Nick more, however, was the cold, casual way in which Yasir had been shot. It didn't bode well for Ruth or PC Garrow. These men had no regard for human life and Nick knew he needed to get them out of there. Fast.

As they hurried to the edge of the compound again, Nick saw Cavendish looking up at the house. There were various lights on inside. Nick knew that in about ten yards, their movement would set off the security lights that would flood the compound with light. But time was running out.

'How well do you know the layout inside?' Cavendish asked.

'I can find my way around the ground floor and some of the first floor,' explained Nick.

Cavendish scanned the entire area. He pointed to the security lights. 'We could do with getting rid of those lights somehow.'

Nick remembered the box with wires he had seen in the space above the garage. 'I think I've seen the fuse box for the house.'

'You sure? It's a safe house, so my guess would be that it is well hidden,' Cavendish said.

'There's a gap above the garage ceiling. It's in there. You would have to know it's there to access it.'

Cavendish nodded. 'Sounds good. If we can pull the power, then most of the house goes into darkness. There's an emergency generator for some lighting and the locks. But most of the house will be pitch black. And that'll be a great leveller if we're going inside.'

'I'll show you,' Nick said, as they moved swiftly around the perimeter of the compound, keeping within the dark shadows of the trees. As he looked up, he saw two dark shapes flapping, moving silently through the sky.

'Bats?' Cavendish asked, as he spotted them too. 'Not a good omen.'

As they continued, Nick's gaze was fixed on the house. He didn't want anyone surprising them again.

'There was an open window on the first floor. I saw it at the back of the house. I'm not sure if we can get in that way?' Nick said.

'If we can pull the power, we'll take a look,' Cavendish replied.

Approaching the garage, Nick clicked on the LED torch. They were now out of the sightlines of the main house. The garage door was still slightly raised. Sliding onto his back, Nick edged himself under the door and into the garage. Cavendish followed him.

As they got up, Cavendish pulled a face. 'Strong smell of petrol?'

'That was me. I chucked some around in case I decided to torch the garage.' Nick gestured to the far corner. 'It's over here.'

Using the torch, Nick walked over to where he had left the stepladder.

Cavendish busied himself by looking at some tools – he grabbed two long screwdrivers. He placed one inside his jacket and then handed the other to Nick.

'Might come in useful,' Cavendish said.

'Thanks,' Nick said.

Climbing to the top of the ladder, Nick pulled himself up into the air vent. He crawled along the shaft for a few yards and then waited for Cavendish to do the same.

Christ, I'm glad I'm not claustrophobic, Nick thought as he looked along the shaft and its roof, which was less than a foot above his head.

They continued to crawl until they reached the part where the air vent had been removed from the garage roof.

The cold, fresh air that swept in from outside was a welcome relief from the thick petrol fumes. Even from here, Nick could smell the pine and spruce from the forest. There was a light at one of the windows of the main house that created a shadowy vanilla-coloured pattern on the floor and wall.

Standing up, Nick pointed to the large grey plastic box on the wall. From the top, white plastic trunking cable stretched up. It looked relatively new and clearly carried all the wiring for the house. 'I'm no electrician, but I'm sure that's the central fuse box.'

Cavendish walked over, flipped the grey cover up to reveal a series of fuses that related to each part of the house. 'We'll soon find out.'

Reaching to the end, Cavendish pushed his finger down on a large black switch.

The safe house was plunged into the darkness of the night. Cavendish then pulled out the whole fuse.

'I hope that works,' Cavendish said.

Suddenly, Nick could hear voices of men shouting. Someone was clearly upset at the electricity being cut.

'I think we have our answer,' Nick said.

Cavendish nodded. 'That will keep them occupied for a bit.'

Nick heaved himself out of the hole where the air vent been removed, and regained his balance on the garage roof. As he steadied himself, he could see he was standing in a trough that ran the length of the roof. However, as his feet moved, the tiles on either side cut into his ankles. With this new pain, he realised that he had now become used to the throbbing of his broken toes.

From here, Nick's eyes adjusted to the night, and the outline of the safe house became clear. The lights had definitely gone. However, the thought of getting inside, then navigating the house in pitch black while avoiding at least two armed men was terrifying. He didn't have a choice. It was either that or sit and wait until someone at Llancastell CID, Special Branch, or MI5 noticed that there had been no contact from anyone. That might not even happen until the morning.

'You said that you'd seen an open window at the back?' Cavendish whispered.

Nick nodded. 'It's a bit further. It's on the first floor, but we would have to climb down from the roof to get to it,' Nick explained. He hoped that Cavendish would take the lead on this, given his climbing expertise.

Slowly traversing the garage roof, they soon got to the place where it joined the roof of the main building. They stepped across. In front of them, nestled in the roof, was a large skylight. As Nick approached, he could see that the glass had been skilfully removed and placed beside it. There was a drop of about twenty feet to the floor below inside the house. He saw a rope curled on the floor.

'That's how they got in,' Nick said.

Cavendish peered down through the skylight. 'Shame we don't have a rope too.'

'Too high to jump,' Nick said, thinking aloud.

'You'd break your ankle,' Cavendish said.

The clouds shifted away from the moon, and Nick looked up at its bright, reassuring presence that now threw light over the whole area. It was bright enough for Nick to turn off his torch – and that meant they were far less conspicuous.

They moved closer to the edge of the roof. Nick knew they could lower themselves down using a drainpipe and perhaps reach the windowsill of the open window.

Cavendish peered down. He looked up at Nick. 'I can get that fully open with the screwdriver. No problem. You okay to follow me down once it's open and I'm inside?' Cavendish asked.

Nick nodded. 'Yeah'. Normally he would have had serious reservations about climbing off a roof to a first-floor window. But tonight was not normal by any stretch of the imagination. There wasn't another option.

Crouching down, Nick looked into the back garden and a gravel path that snaked its way around the perimeter. Cavendish knelt beside him.

Suddenly, there was a slam as the back door to the safe house opened.

Nick and Cavendish froze.

Shit! We're totally exposed here! Nick thought.

The tall, nervy man with the AK-47 came out onto the path. His feet crunched on the gravel. He had an LED torch, which he flicked across the lawn. If the man turned the torch up to the roof, they would be sitting ducks. They would either have to jump and risk broken bones, as it was at least thirty feet, or try to get back across the roof whilst trying to avoid catching a bullet in the back.

Nick held his breath. The muscles in his thighs were burning with the effort of crouching and keeping still. It was also putting extra pressure on his broken toes.

The man shouted something back to someone inside. He then turned the torch to look at the back of the house. There were more angry shouts.

The torch's beam moved across to just below where they were crouched.

The beam stopped moving.

Nick looked at Cavendish.

Fuck! This is it.

Nick held his breath – jump or run?

Jump, and I break my leg. Run and I get shot. Not much of a choice.

Nick held his breath. The beam moved away for a split second – but then came back again.

Jesus! This is torture. He's going to bloody shoot us!

Just as Nick was about to leap, the beam moved away.

Thank God for that! Nick's pulse was thundering so loudly in his ears, he was surprised no one else could hear it.

The man shouted something else, went back in and closed the door.

Nick and Cavendish let out an audible sigh.

'Fuck!' Nick gasped.

'Jesus, that was far too close for my liking,' Cavendish whispered.

For a few seconds, they just crouched in silence, composing themselves.

Then Nick peered down again to check that the coast was clear. Just over to the right was a large wooden gazebo with benches and chairs beside it. Nick assumed that it was the outside smoking area, used when the safe house was busier.

Standing up and stretching his legs for a few seconds, Nick felt the relief in his muscles and his toes. He then gestured to the guttering and the top of the iron drainpipe.

Nick watched as Cavendish crouched, swung down, and used the pipe and uneven stone surface to climb down the back of the house.

It's like watching bloody Spiderman, Nick thought.

After only a few seconds, Cavendish was standing on the windowsill of the room where the window was open.

Brilliant! Nick thought. *We're in!*

Nick looked down as Cavendish reached into his jacket and took out the screwdriver. He just needed to unhook the window restrictor.

Cavendish looked up. Something must have caught his attention, but Nick couldn't see what.

Crack! Crack! Crack! Crack!

There was an explosion of noise and gunfire.

Cavendish was thrown back from the window in a hail of bullets and glass.

Someone inside the room had shot him with a machine gun.

Cavendish fell and crashed to the ground below.

Jumping back from the roof edge, Nick felt sick. He knew that Cavendish would have been dead before he had hit the ground.

CHAPTER 19

RUTH STILL WASN'T A hundred per cent sure what to make of Abu's claim that he was an undercover police officer. However, she was fairly certain that Islamic terrorists didn't walk around with tracking devices in the heels of their shoes. And how else would Abu know the name of DI Gary Brunton in Special Branch?

The drilling was sporadic, which seemed to indicate that the men were struggling to get the door open. Ruth still froze in panic every time there was a metallic clang, expecting the door to fling wide open, terrified the men would come in and shoot them both dead on the spot.

Suddenly, they were plunged into virtual darkness.

The drilling stopped. The men started shouting.

'The power's gone,' Abu's voice said from the shadows.

The moon outside was bright. Ruth could still make out the silhouette of Abu sitting on the bed.

'Or someone's cut it.' Ruth hoped that it was Nick or PC Garrow.

Please God, let them still be alive somewhere out there!

'Might be easier for us to get out,' Ruth said, thinking aloud. She needed to move fast.

'Except I'm handcuffed to this bed,' Abu said.

Ruth grabbed her cigarette lighter. It bathed the room in a dim orange glow. She took the homemade mirror stick. She put it up to the window in the door. Tilted it to show the reflection of the dark corridor outside. It was empty. At least, as far as she could see, it was empty.

Her pulse began to race. *Get out now, while it's dark,* she thought to herself.

'What can you see?' Abu asked.

'Nothing. I don't think there's anyone out there,' Ruth said.

'My guess is that they've gone to find the fuse box,' Abu said.

'Why didn't the door open? It's got electronic locks,' Ruth asked.

'Stuff like that will be on a separate circuit or generator. Otherwise this wouldn't be much of a safe house, would it?' Abu said.

If Ruth was going to move from the holding cell, it needed to be now. The men weren't outside. The house was in virtual darkness.

'I'm getting out of here,' Ruth said. Her stomach tightened at the thought of going out into the impenetrable black of the house.

'What about me?' Abu asked.

'I'll be back,' Ruth said. She got up with a sense of urgency.

She tapped in the code and pressed the security catch. It released noisily.

She grasped the cold metal of the handle and eased it down. She prayed she was right about there being no one out there.

Here we go ... God help me ...

'Be careful,' Abu whispered.

Ruth nodded. She had no idea if he could see her.

Pulling it towards her centimetre by centimetre, Ruth opened the door. She took a deep breath and then peered out into the long, dark corridor.

It was quiet and utterly still.

She had braced herself for gunfire.

Ruth held her breath. Nothing.

Then, out of the darkness, a figure loomed up in front of her.

Ruth jumped with fright. *Jesus bloody Christ!*

She stepped backwards, retreating into the safety of the cell.

The tall figure reached out in the darkness.

At first, Ruth thought the man was going to strangle her.

'Ma'am. It's me, Jim,' said a quiet voice.

It was PC Garrow.

'Bloody hell, Jim! You scared the shit out of me.' Ruth hissed, relieved she wasn't going to have her head blown off.

'Sorry, ma'am.'

'Never mind.' Ruth had a thought. 'Jim, I need the keys for the handcuffs.' She moved back to the door and opened it wider. 'It's a long story, but Abu is an undercover police officer. He needs to come with us.'

PC Garrow looked suitably confused. He fumbled in his pocket and took out the keys.

Clicking on her cigarette lighter again to gain some extra light, Ruth went over to Abu and unlocked his cuffs.

'Thank you,' Abu said quietly, rubbing his wrist to get the circulation back.

Ruth, Abu and PC Garrow crept quietly out of the holding cell and into the darkness of the corridor.

Suddenly, there was a burst of loud gunfire and the sound of breaking glass from the other side of the house. Ruth's immediate thought was Nick.

'Have you seen DS Evans?' Ruth asked anxiously.

PC Garrow shook his head. 'No, ma'am.'

Ruth motioned for them to follow her down the corridor and into the thick darkness.

CHAPTER 20

7.21 pm
Nick

WITH CAVENDISH DEAD and the open window blown, Nick had to formulate an alternative plan of how to rescue his colleagues. *This is beginning to feel like a suicide mission,* he thought.

He peered at the back door. It was a weak point of entry into the safe house. From what he had seen, the younger man used the door to check on the back of the house at regular occurrences.

If I can cause some kind of distraction, Nick thought, *then I can get inside through that door.*

Going back the way he came, Nick traversed the roof, onto the garage, into the air vent and then dropped down into the garage. Grabbing one can of petrol, Nick crawled back to the air vent and returned to the part of the house roof from where he had seen Cavendish murdered. Gazing down, he saw Cavendish's twisted, dead body below. The black holes in his chest formed a triangle. Around him on the lawn, shards of glass were lit up by the moonlight. They glimmered almost as if there was a vigil of small candles around where Cavendish lay. Nick was determined not to allow Greene and Cavendish's lives to have been lost in vain.

Crouching down, he unscrewed the cap of the petrol can, which gave a little hiss. He immediately smelled the thick vapours, which made him blink with their potency. Leaning over the edge of the roof, he carefully poured the petrol onto the wooden gazebo below. Because of the height at which he was pouring, the petrol splattered noisily onto the wood. Nick stopped for a second. He hoped it couldn't be heard from inside.

Holding his breath, he listened. Nothing. He continued to pour again, watching as the liquid splashed over the patio and the garden furniture. As the can emptied, Nick gave it a shake as the last few drops fell.

Putting the can down to one side, he took out the cigarette lighter he had borrowed from Cavendish.

Searching his pockets, he found a scrap of paper. He twisted it, cupped his hand around the lighter, and lit the paper. After a second or two, the paper burnt with an orange flame. Tossing it over the side of the roof, Nick watched the small, flaming piece of paper swirl in the breeze. It then floated out of sight under the gazebo roof.

He waited.

Nothing.

For fuck's sake, I haven't got time for this! He was exhausted, terrified, and had seen three people shot dead. His fiancée was having a baby without him there, and the likelihood of him ever seeing his child was getting smaller by the minute. The world had become a surreal, detached place for him. He just wanted – no, *needed* – to survive.

Vump!

Suddenly, the petrol and its fumes caught with a loud *whoosh*. Within seconds, the entire structure of the gazebo was ablaze with bright orange flames.

Nick felt the wall of heat rush past his face and he stumbled backwards.

That's more like it! he thought.

Satisfied that the blaze would cause enough distraction, he turned and made his way back across the roof. He arrived at the point where the roof was directly above the back door, and waited.

Come on, come on, you fuckers.

As if on cue, Nick heard the door open. There was the sound of agitated shouting.

Peering carefully over the roof's edge, he watched the younger man walk over to the fire, shouting to someone inside the house. He ran back into the house and then reappeared carrying a fire extinguisher. As he tried to put out the fire, Nick knew it was time to make his move.

Lowering himself slowly down, he grabbed the drainpipe. He reached down with his foot to find a suitable foothold. All the time, he focussed his gaze on the young man. If he turned back now, Nick would be seen and shot. Dropping down again, Nick came past the first floor and then leapt the last ten feet. The sound of the fire drowned out the sound of his feet on the gravel.

Glancing around, he edged towards the back door. The young man had left it open by about a foot.

Moving slowly through the door, Nick stopped for a second and listened. He had no idea whereabouts Ruth was in the house. Nor where the other armed man was. And what about the fourth man Yasir had mentioned? Was he armed? And where the hell was PC Garrow?

Working his way through the ground floor, Nick had to move slowly. Inside the building, not much moonlight entered in through the windows; his surroundings were pitch black. With his right hand, he felt the wall and tried to remember the layout of the house.

As he progressed, Nick became aware that up ahead was a hue of red light. It must be the emergency lighting that came on when the power went out. It was probably attached to a separate generator.

With each step, Nick stopped, holding his breath and listening. He cursed his pulse, which pounded in his ears and prevented him from hearing.

He took another few steps and began to make out the hallway. It was bathed in the dim scarlet back-up lighting.

Nick's blood ran cold as he heard the thundering of footsteps. Someone was there. Crouching and glancing up, he could see the figure of a man running down the stairs. He looked anxious. Shining his torch erratically left and right, he was terrified.

Nick walked backwards very slowly, treading carefully so as not to make a sound. As he came back down the corridor, he spotted a thin strip of insipid moonlight shining through a door that was open two inches. He moved across the hallway, his feet light and soft on the carpet.

Opening the door gradually, Nick could see it was some kind of conference room. The shape of a large oval table surrounded by chairs. The light from the moon outside gave the room a tinge of indigo.

Suddenly, there was a sound from behind. Someone was coming. He moved swiftly into the room, dropped to the carpet and crawled under the table. It smelled plasticky – like the smell of new offices.

Looking out from under the table, Nick saw the door open further. He froze, hardly daring to breathe.

Then two military boots appeared. The torch swept around the room for a few seconds.

Then the wearer of the boots came in and began to make a thorough search.

CHAPTER 21

7.21 pm
Ruth

IN THE DARKNESS OF the first floor, Ruth, PC Garrow and Abu crept down the corridor away from the holding cell. Ruth knew that Kashif and Hamzar were relatively far away – they had been shouting out to each other in sporadic bursts for the last ten minutes. There was enough distance between them and the voices to move with relative safety – at least for the meantime.

'You still have the keys I gave you?' Ruth asked PC Garrow as they moved past each door.

'Yes, ma'am. I'm sorry I didn't have time to get outside,' he replied in the darkness.

'Don't worry. I'm just glad you're okay,' she said.

Up ahead, Ruth could see some kind of dim red light. It was at the end of the corridor where the large staircase led down to the ground floor.

The shouts had now stopped, which made Ruth nervous. Kashif and Hamzar could be moving around the house now. And if they were headed back to the holding cell, they would be walking straight towards them.

Ruth tried to speed up, but it was too dark. She caught her knee on the wooden frame of a door. The noise seemed to echo down the corridor and made everyone flinch for a second.

Shit! That hurts.

Suddenly, the light in the hallway dimmed.

They all froze.

A figure had appeared and was blocking out the light. The black silhouette moved down the corridor towards them.

Oh, God. We need to hide.

Ruth was thankful that they would be invisible in the blackness.

Someone tapped her on the shoulder. Widening her eyes to take in as much light as possible, Ruth saw Abu gesturing to a toilet door that was slightly open. He pushed it open slowly.

It was hard for Ruth to get her head around the fact that Abu was a police officer of the same rank as her.

Suddenly, the approaching figure turned on a powerful LED torch. Its beam illuminated the whole corridor.

Bloody hell! They were definitely visible now, weren't they? Now what?

Ruth felt herself being pulled by the shoulder. She lurched backwards into the toilets. She turned and pushed the door so that it was virtually closed. The three police officers stood in the tense silence. Ruth hoped that whoever was walking down the corridor would go straight past.

As the clouds moved away from the moon, the cubicles, sinks and urinals became more visible. It was colder than the rest of the house and it smelled of disinfectant.

Ruth tried to piece together what had happened. It was so worrying not knowing if Nick was all right. What about the MI5 agents that were supposed to have arrived about an hour ago? What had happened to them? And the sporadic gunfire? Were the MI5 agents armed too? She had seen both Kashif and

Hamzar outside the holding cell, so she knew they were both alive.

Abu, who was crouched by the door, put up his hand to signal that the person was now close by. Fragments of light from the torch flickered under the door and through the gap by the doorframe.

The person stopped.

Ruth held her breath and froze.

Her heart was pumping so loudly that she thought it would give them away.

Squinting at the door, she saw that it was beginning to open. The torchlight moved up and down the wall.

That's it! We're totally fucked now.

They would have to jump the person coming in – however dangerous that was.

Suddenly, there was a loud bang from outside.

The room filled with orange and yellow light.

Ruth could immediately smell petrol and smoke.

There were loud shouts from somewhere. The torchlight vanished from the doorway, followed by the sound of footsteps running away.

What the hell was going on?

As they moved to the toilet window, Ruth peered down to the garden and patio. The wooden gazebo she had seen earlier was engulfed in a ball of flames.

'Jesus!' gasped PC Garrow.

'That's not accidental,' Abu mumbled.

Ruth knew that whoever had started the fire had caused a distraction – and probably saved their lives.

CHAPTER 22

7.25 pm

HIDING UNDER THE TABLE, Nick held his breath. The torchlight flicked around the room again. All he could see clearly was the man's black combat boots and a hand hanging by his knee that appeared to be holding a Beretta handgun. Nick's pulse was thudding so loudly and so fast that he thought his heart might explode.

As he lay there on the floor, inches away from fate, Nick pictured Amanda's face in his mind. She could be in full labour by now, for all he knew. His child was being born and he was cowering under a table like a scared cat. Nick swelled with anger. If he was gonna go, it wasn't going to be like this. His newborn child was going to be proud of him. Nick wasn't about to creep around the house only to get killed. He needed to do something – to take control. If he was going down, he was going down fighting.

With a rush of adrenaline, he crawled slowly to the end of the table. He reached in his pocket for the screwdriver that Cavendish had handed him back in the garage. It wasn't there. It must have dropped out somewhere. Now Nick had no weapon of any kind.

He sat crouched. If he headed to the left of the table, he would have a clear ten-yard run at the man. He had played rugby for North Wales; he knew how to tackle someone hard and really hurt him. Although, there weren't many rival rugby players that carried a Beretta.

Fuck this! I'm taking this bastard down!

Nick moved from under the table and, leaping from his crouched position, he broke into a sprint. His opponent had no time to react. Launching himself, Nick hit the man's knees, pulling them together at the same time. The man went flying and crashed noisily to the floor.

Nick was on him before the guy had time to work out what had happened. Punching him hard in the face, Nick got astride him. He punched him again and felt the warmth of blood on his knuckles. The man groaned. Nick punched him again but hit him in the temple. The bone cracked against Nick's knuckles.

In the darkness, Nick couldn't see much. As he pulled back for another punch, he focussed his eyes and realised he was looking down the barrel of the Beretta. Pointed at his face.

Nick didn't know how the guy had kept hold of his weapon when he'd tackled him, but he wasn't going to give him a chance to use it.

Gripping the man's arm, Nick tried to push the gun out of the way. He was stronger than Nick had anticipated. The gun's barrel came back to point at his face again.

Bang!

Nick flinched.

But there was no white-hot pain. No blackness of total annihilation. He was alive. If only just.

The bullet had skimmed the top of his hair as it whistled over his head.

Nick had completely lost the hearing in his left ear, which now sang with a high-pitched ringing.

Using his knee, Nick pinned the man's left arm to the floor. Now he could take his right arm, which held the gun, with both hands. They wrestled. With an almighty push, the man's arm crashed to the floor and the handgun went flying.

In the back of Nick's mind, he knew that the gunshot would have alerted the thick-set man that something was wrong. He would be here quickly. And with the missing AK-47. That wasn't good.

Nick held down the now empty hand, and the man grunted as he struggled. Nick clamped his hand around his throat. He squeezed it with everything he had. The man choked and shook.

For a second, the man looked directly into Nick's eyes. Was Nick able to do this? Kill a man with his bare hands while looking him in the face?

There was no alternative. He had to live to see his child.

As Nick continued to crush the man's throat, he felt the burn of the muscles in his hand.

Come on, come on. Pass out or something.

Nick wasn't sure how long it took to strangle someone, but he had to hold on.

As the man fought and squirmed under him, Nick could feel his protestations getting weaker - strength ebbing away from his opponent's body. The man was gasping as his eyes widened. He shook again violently. Nick looked away. He gripped tighter.

Time seemed to stand still.

Then he felt the body under him relax.

Nick took his hand from his throat and thought about what he had done.

The man's eyes were still wide open – but he was dead.

Nick didn't have time to ponder on this. He scrabbled around on the floor until he found the Beretta. He unclipped the magazine and saw there was only one bullet left. It would have to do.

Getting to his feet, Nick composed himself and headed towards the door. What he had just done would live with him for ever. He knew that.

CHAPTER 23

7.26 pm

AFTER A FEW MINUTES, Ruth was confident that the fire would be keeping Kashif and Hamzar occupied outside. She led the others out of the toilets and down the corridor towards the staircase. Her plan was to get to the surveillance room. She hoped that, like the holding-cell door, some of the CCTV cameras would be on a secure, separate circuit to the main house. From there, she could survey the house and check where Kashif and Hamzar were. Hopefully, she could also check the outside cameras for any signs of what had happened, any clues to the sporadic gunfire, and where Nick might be.

Ruth was focussed. Once they found Nick, they could get out of there. She didn't know about the MI5 agents, but Nick was her priority. As they got to the top of the staircase, Ruth stopped and listened. Was there any movement from downstairs?

From a distance, the sound of a man's voice calling. It sounded like someone was shouting, 'Kashif?' But the voice was distant. Ruth motioned to the others to follow her down the stairs.

As they crept down the staircase, she could see that the central hallway was bathed in the dim scarlet glow they'd seen earlier. It must have been the emergency lighting from when the

power had been cut. It made the second half of the staircase easier to navigate.

At the bottom of the steps, Ruth signalled that they needed
to cross the hallway. The door to the surveillance room was
open by about six inches. She pushed the door very gently.
It began to open. Already she could see the red emergency
lighting was on in there too, but tinged with the blue light of
CCTV and security camera monitors. *They are still on, thank
G—*

'You took your time, didn't you?' A voice came out of the
darkness.

It was Nick.

'Where the hell have you been?' Ruth whispered. She was
overwhelmed with relief.

'A very long story,' Nick said as he got up out of the chair
and came out into the light. His face was smeared with dirt,
blood, and cuts. 'I'm just glad you're okay. Did they hurt you?'

'No, no, I'm fine. I'll tell you everything when we get out
of here,' Ruth said, as she put her hand on Nick's arm. 'I'm glad
you're okay too.'

Nick gestured to Sameer's body that was slumped beside
the table on the far side of the room. 'What happened to him?'

'He got in the way when Jim was rescuing me,' Ruth explained, giving PC Garrow a reassuring nod. He had been
through a lot and the way he had handled himself was impressive.

Nick gestured to the monitors. 'In that case, I think there's
only one of them left, and he's on the other side of the house.'

Ruth looked and saw the grainy image of Hamzar walking
with his torch. He was carrying the AK-47. 'Where's Kashif?'

'Tall, young bloke?' Nick asked.

'His name is Kashif Dallal. He's Iranian, came over to the UK a few months ago,' Abu said.

'Who asked you?' Nick snapped.

Oh God, I've got to try to explain this too.

'Nick, this is Detective Inspector Abu Mallik of the North West Counterterrorism Unit,' Ruth said.

'What? Are you kidding me?' Nick asked, his eyes widening.

'No, I'm not. Abu has been working undercover for the past three years,' Ruth explained.

Nick looked thoroughly confused. 'I don't understand. What did we bring you up here for?'

'I needed to debrief MI5 on what happened yesterday in Manchester,' Abu explained. 'No one foresaw that they were going to try to get to me.'

'Jesus Christ! You're telling me I've almost been killed several times tonight because Special Branch couldn't get their act together? That's pathetic!' Nick snapped.

Abu didn't rise to Nick's outburst. 'What happened to Kashif?' Abu asked.

'We don't need to worry about him,' Nick said with a meaningful look.

'There's another man. Yasir?' Ruth said.

'Yasir Malek,' Abu informed them. 'Where is he?'

'Yasir disappeared somewhere. Do you know where he is?' Ruth asked Nick. There was so much she needed to know, but right now she only needed the information that would help them get out of here.

'He's dead too.' Nick pointed to the image of Hamzar on the CCTV monitor. 'This psycho here shot him earlier.'

'He's Hamzar Mousa. Nasty piece of work,' Abu said.

'How the hell did that happen?' Ruth asked.

'We tried to trade this Yasir for you and Jim's safe return,' Nick said.

'What happened?' Ruth asked.

'They didn't have an exchange policy.'

'The MI5 agents?' Ruth asked.

Nick looked at her. 'They're both dead.'

Oh my God ... What a bloody mess! Ruth tried to comprehend the enormity of everything that had happened.

'We should get out of here,' Abu said in a concerned voice. 'The car we came in isn't far from the door.'

He's starting to sound like a DI, Ruth thought. In fact, since they came out of the holding cell, Abu's whole demeanour and body language had changed. He no longer had to play the part of an Islamic terrorist.

'Have you got the keys, Jim?' Ruth asked with a sense of urgency.

Jim quickly fished them out of his pocket. 'Thanks. If we can open the gates, we can make a run for the car while Hamzar is occupied.'

Nick shook his head. 'No point. They've slashed the tyres.'

'Shit! How do we get out of here then?' Ruth asked anxiously.

Nick held up a handgun. 'The good news is that I've got this. The bad news is that it only has one bullet in it. The first thing to do is for me to get to the two Glocks in the Astra.'

Ruth handed the car keys to Nick.

'Be quick but be careful,' Ruth said. Her pulse was still pounding.

'You've got two Glocks in the car?' Abu asked.

'Yeah. Have you used one before?'

Abu nodded, 'A couple of times. Only on the range.'

'That doesn't help us get out of here, unless we go on foot,' Ruth said.

'The men came in a van but I don't have the keys,' Nick said. 'Otherwise, it's five miles down to the road, or across country. Possibly with a psychopath carrying an AK-47 chasing us.'

'I've seen them,' Ruth said in a hurried tone. 'They're in that kit bag.' She'd remembered seeing some vehicle keys briefly in the tussle between PC Garrow and Sameer when Sameer had reached for the machete.

PC Garrow rushed over, opened the bag, and fished out what looked like a set of van keys. 'Here you go, sir.'

'Thanks, Jim,' Nick said, taking the keys and jogging to the door. 'Once I've got the Glocks, I'll go and see if I can get the van.'

Ruth looked at him. 'Be careful, Nick.'

'When am I ever not careful?'

'You really want me to answer that?' Ruth said, watching him go.

Ruth glanced at PC Garrow. He looked surprisingly calm for such a young officer.

'You okay, Jim?' Ruth asked in a gentle voice.

'I think so,' was the uncertain reply.

'You're doing a grand job. Although I bet you're regretting telling me that you'd prefer something more challenging,' Ruth said with a dark sardonic smile.

He nodded. 'Yeah, I could have done with sitting and reading a book tonight.'

'Hang on in there, okay?' Ruth said in an encouraging tone.

Ruth went to the monitors where Abu was scanning them – he looked worried.

'Everything okay?' Ruth asked, sensing his unease.

'I'm not sure,' Abu said.

'Where's Hamzar?' Ruth asked.

'That's the thing. He went outside, but now I've lost him.'

CHAPTER 24

7.48 pm

CLICKING OPEN THE FRONT door, Nick exited the safe house. He stopped and checked that the safety catch on the Beretta was off. He hoped that he didn't have to use it; he was so done with all this running around. And for what? Their prisoner wasn't even a prisoner at all! Shaking his head, Nick scanned left and right, but couldn't see anyone.

The clouds drifted away from the moon and the compound glistened in its light. Nick walked down each step slowly, his weapon drawn – he wasn't taking any chances. It was probably only fifty yards to where the Astra was parked. He could sprint it in about ten to twenty seconds. Maybe a bit longer, given the way he was feeling – although he could no longer feel his broken toes.

When he had seen Ruth walk into the surveillance room, he'd been awash with such an acute sense of relief knowing she was all right. His own rescue operation had hardly gone to plan, and with each passing minute he'd worried even more about the likelihood that the men might have resorted to torturing her if they'd needed the code for the holding cell.

A slight breeze swirled around his face as he placed his feet onto the bottom step. Still no sign of Hamzar.

Breaking into a slow jog, Nick crunched over the gravel. He had barely any energy left in his legs. Scanning around again, he could see that the coast was clear. He stopped at the car. Opening the door, he put the gun down on the driver's seat. He fumbled in his pockets for the car keys. Pulling them from his pocket, he heard a sound.

Glancing left, he couldn't see anything. He put the keys down on the driver's seat, while he went to lift the sliding plate that exposed the lock for the armoury. He thought of the two Glocks inside.

Crack! Crack! Crack!

Thunderous clamour of gunfire.

A split second later, Nick felt as if someone had hit him in the back of his left shoulder with a sledgehammer. He went flying and fell face-first into the gravel.

Then a piercing, white-hot pain in his shoulder.

He had been shot.

Trying to get his breath, Nick rolled on the gravel drive. He could see Hamzar was approaching fast.

Crack! Crack!

Two bullets punched holes in the door of the Astra.

If I don't get up and get moving, I'm a dead man.

Scrambling towards the open door, Nick lunged towards the driver's seat. He grabbed the Beretta. His shoulder screamed. His left arm felt weak.

Crouching down behind the door, Nick peered around to see that Hamzar was only thirty yards away.

One shot, mate. You've got one shot, make it count.

Going down low, Nick took a breath. With the gunshot and the adrenaline, he was feeling physically sick.

Fuck it, here goes.

Nick dropped to the gravel and watched from under the door.

At first, Hamzar didn't see him – he was expecting Nick to come behind the door higher up.

Closing his left eye, Nick pointed the gun at Hamzar. His hand was shaking. He had no strength in his left hand to help keep the gun steady. But he had one shot.

Hamzar spotted Nick and gave fire.

Crack! Crack!

The bullets smashed into the ground in front of Nick, throwing sharp gravel into his face. He nearly dropped the gun.

Jesus Christ!

Blinking the grit out of his eyes, Nick focussed again. If Hamzar shot again, he wouldn't miss.

Nick aimed, breathed in and prayed. He squeezed the trigger.

Bang!

Hamzar continued to walk towards him.

Fuck! Missed!

Just as Nick tried to think of what to do next, Hamzar crumpled to the ground and lay motionless.

Nick had no idea where the bullet had gone – he still wasn't sure he'd hit Hamzar – but he wasn't moving. Taking a breath, Nick got on his knees and then stood up. He kept his gaze on Hamzar's body that lay about twenty-five yards away.

Nick wondered if they needed the Glocks now if Hamzar was dead and all four intruders accounted for. He would take the guns anyway. He could go and get the others from inside the house. He would then lead them to the van and make their escape.

For the first time in over an hour, Nick felt some sense of hope. He took a deep breath and could feel his pulse starting to slow.

Resting his throbbing arm on the top of the car door, Nick caught sight of something out of the corner of his eye.

Hamzar was sitting up and was trying to get to his feet.

Come on! You are fucking joking, aren't you? This is like some terrible film!

Glancing down at the armoury compartment and the keys, Nick realised that he didn't have time to get the Glocks out. Hamzar would shoot him.

Crack! Crack!

Two bullets hit the car's windscreen, which then exploded and glass flew in every direction.

Nick tried to make a run for it. He had no energy.

I'm going to get shot in the back!

Glancing back, Nick could see that Hamzar was limping.

I must have only shot him in the leg. Bollocks.

Crack!

Hamzar shot again as Nick ran as fast as his body would take him. He couldn't go back inside the house. That's where everyone else was. Where now?

I'm running aimlessly.

Then Nick had a thought. Was there anything in the garage that he could use? A nail gun? Anything to even things up a bit.

Crack!

A bullet flew beside his head. It was so close that he heard it whizz past his left ear.

Ducking right from the driveway, Nick headed for the side of the house where the garage was. He tried to weave as he ran, to make himself a harder target to hit. However, the pain in his shoulder was making it hard to run at all.

He ran up the slight slope and reached the garage door. Trying to catch his breath, he glanced back. Hamzar was still hobbling, but he wasn't far away. Maybe fifty yards.

Nick looked down at the garage door – it still had a two-foot gap at the bottom. Getting onto his knees, he laid down on his back. Pain seared through his shoulder as the pressure of his bodyweight pushed it into the ground.

Crack!

A bullet clanged against the garage door just above his head. The whole door shuddered with the vibrations.

Shuffling on his back under the door, Nick grimaced and let out a groan.

He was now inside the garage. Rolling onto his right-hand side, Nick got onto his knees and then used his last remaining reserves of strength to stand up. He sucked in a breath to try to counteract the pain, but his desperate need for fresh air was countered by the petrol fumes that hit his nostrils.

Petrol fumes ... He had another idea.

Glancing towards the back of the garage, Nick could see that the stepladder was still where he had left it. Trying to break into a jog, he pulled off his jacket, which was now soaked in blood. He threw it to one side – it was weighing him down and restricting his movements.

He got to the stepladder only to see Hamzar's shadow appear underneath the garage door. Gripping the cold steel, Nick climbed the steps. His entire body was shaking. There was a sound from the garage door – Hamzar was edging his way underneath.

Reaching the top of the steps, Nick looked at the gap in the ceiling. How the hell was he going to pull himself up there? Glancing back, he could see Hamzar sliding under the garage doors.

Either you pull yourself up there, or you'll die.

Nick reached up with his right arm. There was no way he could pull himself up with one arm. He would have to use his left arm and somehow bear the pain. Pushing his left arm up, he gripped the edge around the space in the ceiling.

Trying to take more of the weight on his right arm, Nick felt the searing white heat of agony shoot through his left shoulder. It took his breath away.

Crack! Crack!

A bullet hit the stepladder, smashing it away from under him.

All Nick's bodyweight now hung on his arms. He pulled with everything he had. The pain in his shoulder was so intense that he thought he was going to pass out.

Come on!

With a final burst of strength from somewhere deep inside, Nick pulled himself up and into the cavity above the garage ceiling. It was thick with petrol fumes, which made it hard to breathe and get enough oxygen.

Crack! Crack!

A bullet smashed through the ceiling, missing his right leg by an inch.

Scrambling forward on his elbows, Nick pushed with his legs with every last bit of strength he had left.

He somehow reached the air vent without Hamzar's erratic shots through the ceiling turning him into a cheese grater. Ripping his shirt off, he reached into his pocket and pulled out Cavendish's cigarette lighter.

Suddenly, Hamzar's head appeared at the other end of the air vent.

Shit!

Clicking the lighter, Nick lit the bottom of his bloody shirt. It took a few agonising seconds to catch. Then the orange flame took hold of the material.

Crouching down, Nick took the flaming shirt and tossed it back down into the long ceiling cavity that he had just crawled along. He burnt his hand, but he was now past caring.

His eyes met Hamzar's.

That one look said everything.

Nick watched as Hamzar realised exactly what was going to happen. And there was no way out.

It was too late.

Nick turned, took two steps and dived out of the open air vent.

He crashed hard onto the garage roof.

Vump!

A gigantic ball of orange flame filled the ceiling cavity and swirled out of the open vent. The wall of heat exploded up-wards as flames rolled up into the air. A thick cloud of jet black smoke followed them.

The petrol fumes inside the ceiling cavity had ignited – and Hamzar was now, quite literally, toast.

Nick got up and ran across the roof, his feet slipping on the tiles. He knew what was going to happen next.

Bang!

The whole ground shook with a huge explosion. The fumes and petrol in the garage had ignited too. Some tiles on the garage roof lifted into the air with the force of the blast.

Nick turned to see that the garage and its roof behind him were engulfed in fire and smoke.

He crouched down and drew in a deep, long breath. The pain from his gunshot wound was sharp and overwhelming, so much so that he could hardly see straight. With his shirt now off, Nick inspected the wound. There was a nasty gash at the top of his left shoulder that was covered in blood. From what he could see, the bullet had grazed the top of his shoulder but hadn't travelled through anything vital. It could have been much worse.

Slumping down to the floor, Nick collapsed onto his back, wiping the black soot and dirt from his eyes. To his left, the structure of the garage was consumed in thick, noisy flames. He could feel the heat from where he lay on the roof of the house.

Casting his gaze skywards, Nick looked long and hard at the moon that had dropped low in the black sky. He didn't know if it was his imagination, but the crimson hue seemed to have vanished from its face, as if someone had wiped it clean.

CHAPTER 25

8.04 pm

RUTH'S BODY TENSED when she heard the explosion outside. She turned to look at PC Garrow and Abu, both of whom looked equally frightened, and they all ran to the door. Hamzar must have ambushed Nick. But by the time she peered outside, the two men had vanished. She feared the worst. Nick had one bullet and Hamzar had a machine gun. It wasn't an even match.

Stepping cautiously down the steps, Ruth scanned left and right but she couldn't see anything. The windscreen of the Astra was smashed and the doors were open and littered with bullet holes, but both men were nowhere to be seen. PC Garrow and Abu joined her.

'Any sign of them?' Abu asked.

'No. Nothing,' Ruth said. She wracked her brain for what to do. Nick could be in a great deal of danger, but she didn't know where the bloody hell he'd gone.

Abu pointed left towards the perimeter wall. 'Maybe he went that way to get the van?'

PC Garrow looked at Ruth. 'Wait there, ma'am.'

'Where are you going?' Ruth asked.

But PC Garrow was already off and running. He was heading for the Astra that was parked on the drive beside some bushes about fifty yards away.

When Garrow arrived at the car, he turned and waved at her. She turned to Abu, who shrugged, and, looking left and right in case Hamzar was hiding out with his machine gun, both officers jogged to join the young constable.

'What's going on?' Ruth said, a little out of breath as she arrived at the car. She blamed the anxiety of the situation as opposed to the cigarettes and lack of fitness.

PC Garrow bent into the vehicle and withdrew a set of keys from the front seat. 'Are these the right keys, ma'am?'

'Yes,' Ruth said.

She watched as PC Garrow went to the passenger side of the car and crouched into the footwell. He slid the metal plate, wiggled in the key and released the lock on the armoury.

Ruth's senses were heightened. It was vital that they retrieve the guns, but she felt like a sitting duck, exposed in the open like this. There was still no sign of Nick and no clues as to where he was.

Where the hell is he?

PC Garrow came over with the two black Glock 9mm handguns.

Finally.

There was no time to waste.

Taking the guns, she approached Abu and handed one to him. 'Right, Detective Inspector, we need to go and find Nick.'

Abu looked at her and gestured. 'I don't think we need to anymore.'

Ruth looked over and saw a bedraggled figure approaching. It was Nick. He was hobbling, shirtless, and covered in blood and dirt. She could see a wound on his left shoulder.

'Bloody hell! Nick!' Ruth said as she ran to him.

'It's all right, boss. I'm okay ... just,' Nick said weakly.

'Your shoulder?' Ruth said.

'I think it's just a flesh wound. Hurts like hell, but it's not going to kill me.' Ruth helped him to the Astra where Abu and PC Garrow were still standing.

'What happened to Hamzar Mousa?' Abu asked.

Nick gestured back to the garage. 'Whatever is left of him is back in the garage.'

'Now are we sure there is no one left? I'm not in the mood for any more surprises,' Ruth said, both joking and deadly serious. It had been a bloody long night.

'That's the lot of them.' Nick gritted his teeth. He was in a lot of pain. Time to go home.

Knowing that all the men that had come to capture Abu were now dead, Ruth took a deep breath. It felt like coming up from being submerged underwater, and she could finally breathe. She allowed herself to bathe in the relief.

'Shall we get us to this van, then?' Ruth asked. 'We can clean you up inside first if you want,' she said, gesturing to the house.

'No, I just want to get out of here,' Nick said.

'We need to get you looked at as soon as possible — Oh my God, Amanda!' Ruth said, with the sudden realisation that she had forgotten that Nick might become – or already be – a father any time now.

'I spoke to her before all this kicked off. Her waters broke this afternoon,' Nick explained.

Ruth put her Glock on the roof of the car and held her hand out. It was visibly shaking. 'Unless anyone minds, I'm going to have a ciggie before we do anything.'

'I would warn you they are dangerous, ma'am, but after tonight ... do you have a spare?' PC Garrow asked, allowing himself a smile.

Ruth smiled back at him. 'Yeah, I think after tonight anything goes, doesn't it?'

There were smiles all round. As she lit her cigarette, Ruth watched Abu collect her gun from the roof of the car and put it with his own gun, presumably to put them somewhere safe.

Ruth gestured to her coat and looked at Nick. 'Are you cold, Nick?'

'No, no. Still running off an adrenaline jacket. And I don't think I'm going to complain about surveillance being boring ever again,' Nick said with a grin.

'I will take boring every time now,' Ruth said with a nod as she blew the smoke from her cigarette. She wanted to get home, have a hot bath, a very strong drink, and a blissful sleep. However, before all that she would be in a series of debriefs with North Wales Police's top brass. Two MI5 officers had lost their lives tonight in the line of duty.

Ruth watched as Nick went to the boot of the Astra, took out a first-aid kit and a dark blue Nike T-shirt that he kept in there as a spare.

'You'd better give me that,' PC Garrow said, gesturing to the first-aid kit.

'You know what you're doing?' Nick said, half joking.

'First-aid trained, but I don't think I can do much more than bandage it up.'

'No end to your talents, Jim,' Ruth said. It felt a little strange to say anything humorous given the evening they'd had.

'I think it's stopped bleeding,' Nick said, inspecting the wound. He then pulled on his T-shirt, wincing a little.

'At least you'll have a scar to show Evans Junior,' Ruth said with a smile as she stubbed out her ciggie with her foot. 'Okay, let's get go—'

She felt something push against her left temple. It was metallic, cold and hard.

'Sorry to break up the party, but there's been a change of plan,' said a voice behind her.

It was Abu.

He had pushed the barrel of a Glock into the side of her head.

'What are you talking about?' Ruth asked.

'I can't let any of you leave here alive tonight,' Abu said.

'What the hell is going on?' Nick said angrily, moving towards Abu.

'Stay there or I'll blow her head off,' Abu snapped, moving further behind Ruth so she couldn't see him. In a deliberate display of power, he clicked off the safety catch.

Is this actually happening?

'What the bloody hell are you doing?' Ruth yelled, trying to make sense of things. 'You're a police officer.'

'Yes, you are right. I am a detective inspector in the North West Counterterrorism Unit,' Abu said. 'And I have been working undercover within the Islamic Alliance terror network for the past three years.'

It was unnerving to hear Abu's voice behind her but not see his face.

'So why are you holding a gun to her head?' Nick growled.

'Except I have been working for the Islamic Alliance for seven years, and I've never stopped being part of them,' Abu said.

Ruth didn't understand what Abu was talking about. It sounded like a riddle.

The penny dropped. He had been so convincing back in the house.

'You're a double agent,' Nick spat.

Ruth tried to process what was happening, which was difficult with a gun pressed against her head.

Abu was a terrorist who had managed to get himself to the position of detective inspector in the North West Counterterrorism Unit. He had then been used to go undercover in the very terrorist organisation that he was a member of.

Ruth felt sick with the enormity of it all. How many terrorist attacks had the police 'squashed' or how many had they inadvertently assisted?

'You bastard,' Ruth growled. How had she got it so wrong?

'Which is why Special Branch couldn't work out why the terrorist units were always one step ahead,' Nick said, filling in more gaps.

'Big surprise. However, I do think that after what's happened here tonight, my position has been compromised,' Abu admitted.

'So you kill us. Then what? Go on the run?' Ruth said with an angry snort.

'Far from it. I make a phone call as soon as I have a signal. I get picked up. And by tomorrow I will be sitting on a beautiful sandy beach on the North African coast, being waited on hand

and foot as a hero of the Islamic jihad,' Abu boasted. 'But for that to happen, yes, I have to kill you.'

'And you're happy to do that? Do you know what it takes to shoot three human beings in cold blood?' Nick snorted.

'Many of my Muslim brothers have done far braver things,' Abu said.

Abu didn't sound like he was remotely fazed by committing multiple murders, Ruth thought. She still couldn't believe that she had misjudged him. Her instinct was normally spot on.

As the gun was pressed harder to her head, Ruth knew she would be first. To say that she had been through a rollercoaster of emotions that day was a dark understatement.

She breathed slowly and closed her eyes to try to calm her racing mind and figure out what to do. Was there any way out of this? When she opened them, something caught Ruth's eye. Lights in the dark countryside to the left. She tried to focus again, turning her eyes to see whilst keeping her head still so as not to alert Abu behind her. There were headlights moving along the track up to the safe house from the main road.

Ruth felt a spark of hope. Had someone called the safe house and become suspicious when there was no answer? Had Drake, or agents from MI5 and Special Branch, sent officers to investigate? Would they be armed?

Ruth tried to use her eyes to signal to Nick that a vehicle was coming. She could see that he had already spotted it. His face looked drawn and grey, and he was shivering. Even though he wasn't losing a lot of blood now, he had been shot. He might be in some kind of shock.

Ruth knew it wouldn't be long before Abu also saw the approaching headlights.

As the vehicle turned a bend, Ruth could now hear its engine. She felt Abu pull the gun away from her head as he moved backwards and looked towards the approaching vehicle. The engine growled and juddered.

If it was a police unit coming to investigate, it was unlikely they would be prepared for immediate gunfire. As the vehicle got closer, Ruth could see from its outline that it was a van. She hoped it was full of AROs packing submachine guns that would cut Abu clean in half. However, inevitably that's not how these things turned out.

The van slowed down to a crawl as it came through the gates, which must have opened when the power was cut. It didn't look like a police vehicle. Nick shot Ruth a look – *who the hell is that?*

'Keep quiet,' Abu growled. 'Or I'll kill you.' He pressed the gun closer into her head before pulling it away.

'You're going to kill us anyway,' PC Garrow pointed out.

Bloody hell, Jim has got some balls.

Abu ignored him as he stepped forward.

A man got out of the van.

Even from where Ruth was standing, she could see that he had long hair tied into a ponytail.

She didn't recognise him but the vehicle was unmistakeable. It was the black van that had sped past them earlier that morning with the mountain bikes mounted on the rear.

What the hell are they doing here?

'Hi. Is everything all right? We could see the flames from the road but couldn't see any fire engines or lights,' the man shouted. He sounded concerned.

'We're fine,' Abu said, his voice changing to an almost too casual tone as he took a few steps towards him.

Ruth, Nick and PC Garrow were still in the darkness but must have now been visible. Ruth knew that if they shouted out, the couple's lives would also be in danger too. She just wanted them to turn around and get away safely.

'We just wanted to see if everything is okay?' the man said as his girlfriend, who was still wearing the red bandana, got out of the driver's side of the van.

'We called 999 on the way up here,' the girl said, waving her mobile phone. 'We thought it might have been a farm on fire. Is anyone hurt?'

'No, no. Everyone is fine,' Abu said, keeping the Glock out of sight behind his back.

What the hell was Abu going to do? Try to persuade them to go? Shoot them? She then saw Abu's reaction. A phone call to 999 would mean fire engines were on their way, plus a phone call to the North Wales Police main operator.

The man looked around and then over at Ruth, Nick and PC Garrow, who was still in uniform. He frowned. 'Is everything all right here?' His tone was uncertain, as if suspicious.

Then the man spotted Yasir's body lying over by the trees. He backed away towards the van. Ruth could almost see the cogs in his brain working on overtime. He knew there was something very wrong about what he and his girlfriend had stumbled upon.

'Right, okay. Well, if it's all okay, we'll get going,' the man stammered.

It was too late for them to get out of this now.

'Both of you! Get over here! Now! Or I'll shoot you,' Abu said, drawing the Glock from behind his back and pointing it at them.

They both instinctively put their hands up.

'Hey, we don't want any trouble. We'll just go and won't say anything,' the man said – he was clearly terrified.

'Shut up!' Abu then waved the gun at Ruth, Nick and PC Garrow. 'This way. Come on!'

Shepherding them all, Abu got all five people into a group on the driveway. 'Right! Sit down! Everyone sit down!' he yelled aggressively.

Ruth could see that the girl in the bandana had started to cry – she didn't blame her.

'Keys?' Abu said, snapping his fingers at the girl and waving the gun in her face. She was visibly shaking with tears streaming down her face.

'They're ... still in ... the ignition,' she stammered as her boyfriend tried to comfort her.

Ruth glared up at Abu with growing contempt. 'So, what's the plan now? Shoot five innocent people? That takes a lot of guts. A lot of courage.' Ruth sneered.

Abu walked over, grabbed Ruth by the hair and pulled her up to her feet.

He's going to shoot me first. She thought of her parents, and of being a child in Battersea. Of Ella – poor Ella. Of Sarah. And Sian.

Abu was now dragging hard on her hair, and her scalp stung with the force. 'I'm taking you with me as my insurance policy. No one is going to run me off the road or fill the van with bullets while a respected female DI is inside.'

Abu dragged Ruth to the van and slid open the side panel. Inside was an assortment of bike parts, sleeping bags, and climbing equipment.

Pushing Ruth down into the rear seat of the van, Abu glanced back at the others to make sure that they hadn't moved. Over his shoulder, Ruth could see PC Garrow looking over at Nick and gesturing.

As Abu climbed into the van, Ruth looked for an opportunity to tackle him. A moment where his guard was down. As he turned for a second to pull a climbing rope from a hook, Ruth saw her chance. She kicked him in the thighs, hoping that he would lose balance and she could get the gun.

They grappled and took a step outside the van. Ruth smashed his hand on the van, making Abu drop the gun to the ground. In an attempt to stop him from getting it again, Ruth kicked it under the van.

With Abu now unarmed, she might be able to take control of the spiralling situation. However, he spun around angrily, pulled the other Glock from his waistband, and hit her across the temple with its handle.

The side of her head erupted with catastrophic pain, and her vision went sparkly as she worried she might pass out. Blinking, she tried to regain her vision. As her head swam, she felt Abu taking her arms and wrists and tying them behind her back and to the seat with a piece of climbing rope.

Abu pointed the gun at Nick and PC Garrow, who had got up.

'Get back down!' Abu yelled.

By the time she had come back to full consciousness, Ruth couldn't move. She locked eyes with Nick. Was Abu really going to shoot them all in cold blood?

Suddenly, PC Garrow sprang to his feet.

What's he doing?

PC Garrow walked towards Abu, who was now outside the van.

'Stay there!' Abu yelled at him.

'If you think I'm going to sit here quietly while you shoot us all, you'd better think again,' PC Garrow sneered as he continued approaching.

'I will shoot you!' Abu shouted.

'Jim!' Ruth shouted.

'Do it! Go on, you cowardly little man! Fucking do it!' PC Garrow sped up his walk.

Jesus! What is he doing? It was a huge gamble to take if Abu wasn't bluffing about killing them all.

'Jim, stay there!' Ruth shouted. 'That's an order.'

Ruth saw Abu's finger move to the trigger.

He's going to shoot Jim in the chest! Oh God!

Click! Click!

Nothing.

There was no shot.

Abu's eyes were wild as he glanced nervously down at the gun – he pulled the trigger again.

Click. Click.

Nothing.

PC Garrow reached into his pocket and pulled out a magazine of bullets. 'Looking for this?' He smiled and broke into a run.

Nick was now up on his feet and sprinting for the van too.

Scrambling with the door, Abu jumped into the driver's seat and started the engine.

Ruth watched helplessly from her seat as PC Garrow sprinted and then launched himself into the back of the van where Ruth was tied up.

The van lurched away and turned hard on the gravel drive.

PC Garrow tried to get up, but as the van twisted at speed, he lost his balance and tumbled out of the van, landing on the ground.

Looking out the front, Ruth stared in alarm as Abu drove the van at high speed out of the compound gates and headed for the main road.

She glanced back through the rear windows at the figures on the drive, silhouetted against the orange flames of the burning garage that spewed a thick plume of black smoke up into the moonlit sky.

CHAPTER 26

WITH THE FULLY LOADED Glock now sitting in his waistband, Nick gestured to the others to follow him.

'How did you know there was something dodgy about Abu Habib?' Nick asked, still aghast at what he had just witnessed the young constable do.

'When DI Hunter couldn't find you, Abu immediately pointed east towards this point of the wall and said you might have gone to get the van. How did he know where the van was parked? You didn't mention where it was. He must have known all the details of the rescue attempt before it had happened, but when he told us he didn't, that made me suspicious,' Garrow explained.

'Bloody hell! Well spotted. And you removed the magazine from a handgun that you then handed to someone you knew to be a detective inspector?' Nick asked.

'DI Hunter told me to go with my instinct. My instinct was not to give him a loaded gun,' Garrow said.

'So you knew which Glock had the bullets and which one didn't the whole time?' Nick asked.

'Sort of,' PC Garrow said with a shrug.

'Sort of? Jesus, and you had the balls to walk straight at him?' Nick said. He wasn't sure he'd have had the courage in the same situation.

'It was fifty-fifty, wasn't it? And I wasn't going to sit there and let him shoot us,' PC Garrow explained.

'I've got to hand it to you, Jim. Impressive stuff,' Nick said.

Knowing roughly where the terrorists' van had been positioned against the compound wall, Nick and PC Garrow, along with the young couple – April and Seb, they had now learned – broke into a jog. They had the keys, but they would be a few minutes behind Abu Habib and Ruth. It was potluck whether they went right or left at the end of the track. Nick's instinct was that if Abu was going to get help to escape the country, he would have to head east towards England. And that meant turning right and heading for the A5.

As they jogged across the edge of the trees, Nick turned back to the young couple who were looking understandably shell-shocked.

'If we can get this van working, I will drop you at the nearest house or petrol station. Okay? Then you'll be safe,' Nick shouted.

Seb merely nodded.

Gazing down at the map that he had pulled from his trousers, Nick looked at the point of the wall that the terrorists had marked with an X.

Then Nick saw a tree that had grown against the wall. It was obvious why the men had chosen this spot. It was a security camera blind spot. Once you were on the wall, you could use the branches to climb down the other side.

'This is it,' Nick said. As he got closer, he could also see that an old, thin mattress had been placed over the wall for protection against the razor wire.

Bingo! This was definitely the right place.

Getting to the tree, Nick looked at PC Garrow. 'Jim, I'll go up first and you can bring up the rear.'

Even though Nick would struggle to pull any weight on his left arm, he could see that the branches were close enough to use his legs. They were essentially a series of large steps.

Having got himself up the tree and on top of the wall, Nick guided Seb and April up the branches. He took their hands as they stepped gingerly across to the wall. From there, they could step down onto the roof of the van and then to the ground.

A few minutes later, Nick had everyone inside the van.

'Bagsy shotgun,' Nick said as he tossed the keys over to PC Garrow. They weren't going to catch up with Abu and Ruth with a one-armed driver.

CHAPTER 27

GLANCING FORWARDS, Ruth had a fairly decent view out of the windscreen and the windows of both the driver and passenger doors. However, it was dark outside. With no street-lights, she was relying on looking for place names, signs, or landmarks that were lit up by the van's headlights.

There was the sound of a mobile phone ringing. Ruth saw Abu take a burner phone from a secret pocket near his crotch.

Answering the phone, he swung the van hard around a long bend. Ruth felt herself being pulled left, as the climbing ropes that held her to the seat cut into her flesh under the strain.

Abu was talking in Arabic. He was animated and excitable. What was he talking about? Or more importantly, what was his next move?

However, Ruth could also see that he was distracted and paying no attention to her. Taking her right foot, she lifted it against the sock on her left leg where she had hidden her phone whilst in the holding cell. Carefully pushing it from the bottom, she used the top of her right foot to ease the phone up the sock so it was now visible. Another inch or two and it would drop beside her feet.

Suddenly, the van tilted hard right – Abu was driving too fast and not concentrating on the road. Ruth looked on, helpless, as her phone swayed in the stretching elastic. If her phone tipped out now, it would go skidding across the van floor and out of reach.

As the van hit a straight stretch of road, Ruth nudged the phone out of the sock. It plopped onto the floor between her feet. She put her left foot on top of it to make sure that it didn't slide anywhere.

But now what?

Looking out of the windscreen, Ruth watched as they zipped past a green road sign. The only thing she managed to read was *Betws-y-Coed – 10 miles.* From her limited knowledge, and from what Nick had told her about the mountain range, Ruth was pretty sure that they were heading north. In fact, they might be heading for the coast.

Watching Abu still talking, she assumed that he was arranging some kind of rescue. Maybe they would take him from the North Wales coast by boat to get him out of the country. It wouldn't be long before he was Britain's most wanted man, and his picture would be on every television station, newspaper, and social media outlet.

Ruth looked down at the phone. Could she use the big toe on her right foot to press some buttons on the pad of her phone? It seemed to be a long shot. She remembered a film about the Irish artist Christy Brown who could paint, type, and write with the toes of his left foot. But he'd had a lifetime of practice.

First, she needed to get the boot off her right foot. Pushing down on the sole with her left boot, she wiggled and loosened her right. Pulling up slowly, she felt the boot hold on to her sock, but her foot came free. Even better.

Stealing a glance, Abu was still listening intently to the phone and nodding.

Ruth hovered her foot above the pad of her smartphone. Pushing down with her big toe, the screen came up requesting her passcode. *1969* – the year of her birth. Ella always told her off for it being too easy for someone else to guess it. She was bloody grateful she could remember it now. Moving her foot down slowly, Ruth managed to press the numbers without accidentally catching the wrong number.

Come on, Ruth. You've got this.

The screen changed to show all her apps. In the top right, she saw the 4G logo.

Thank God! This might just work!

Pushing down carefully on the green phone icon, Ruth saw a page marked *Recents*. Glancing down, she could see the last number she had dialled: *DCI Ashley Drake.*

Right, do not mess this up.

Circling her big toe above the pad again, she tried to touch the contact name. She was about a millimetre above the screen when the van hit a bump. The phone moved, but only about an inch.

Using her feet again, Ruth lowered her big toe and touched the screen. It flicked onto the black screen that read *Calling DCI Ashley Drake.*

Ruth stared at the screen, willing Drake to answer his phone. It kept on ringing. *No, come on. Come on!*

Then, with a flash, the screen switched to show that Drake had picked up her call.

Oh my God!

Abu had finished his call and she could see his eyes glaring at her from the rear-view mirror.

Shit! Can he see what I'm doing? She had to let Drake know what was happening and where she was, without Abu realising what she was doing. If she was caught, she was as sure as dead.

'Where are we going, Abu?' Ruth said in a loud voice, hoping Drake was listening and not thinking that she had butt-called him.

'Shut up!' Abu growled back at her.

'These ropes are really hurting me. Can't you stop and loosen them?' Ruth said.

'If you don't shut up, I will stop and gag you,' Abu snapped.

'So, if we're nearly at Betws-y-Coed, are we going to the coast?' Ruth asked. If Drake was listening, he would realise she was on the main road between the safe house and Betws-y-Coed. It would narrow down her location significantly.

Suddenly a car pulled out of a small turning. Abu slammed on the brakes.

Ruth watched in horror as the mobile phone shot forward and skidded under Abu's driver's seat.

Shit!

CHAPTER 28

RACING ALONG THE A470, Nick had taken a gamble that Abu Habib and Ruth were heading for the A5, the main road east from North Wales. Maybe they were heading north to the coast from there?

PC Garrow floored the van and the engine growled under the strain of the acceleration.

Tapping in the number to Llancastell CID, Nick waited as the phone rang.

Come on, come on!

Nick could hear the call being rerouted to the main switchboard and then, 'Hello? Llancastell Police Station.'

'This is Detective Sergeant Nick Evans. This is an emergency. Detective Inspector Ruth Hunter has been kidnapped by terror suspect Abu Habib. They are in a black Renault van, registration,' Nick glanced down at the piece of paper Seb had scribbled. 'Lima-Yankee-six-three, whisky-alpha-alpha. We believe they are heading north on the A-four-seven-zero, ten miles west of the junction with the A-five. Can you try to get me through to DCI Drake if he's still in the building?' Nick asked.

'Hold the line, DS Evans,' the operator said.

Up ahead, Nick saw a roadside pub. He glanced at PC Garrow. 'Drop them here,' Nick said, pointing. He then turned to look at Seb and April. 'Right, guys, we're going to drop you here. I'll send a patrol car to pick you up and take you back to Llancastell Police Station where I'll need you to write witness statements. I know this has been a rough night for you both, but you've done an amazing job of keeping calm.'

PC Garrow applied the brakes hard, pulling the van to a stop outside the pub. The couple got out and before they had time to say anything, PC Garrow had floored the accelerator and roared away.

Nick still had the phone to his ear when he heard a familiar voice. 'Nick?'

It was Drake.

'Boss?'

'What the hell is going on up there?' Drake asked, sounding very concerned.

'It's too complicated to go into, but—' Nick said.

Drake interrupted him. 'I had a phone call from Ruth's mobile. She said she was tied up and heading for Betws-y-Coed. She said the name Abu, so I assumed she was talking to Abu Habib. Then the phone went dead.'

'Ruth's been kidnapped by Abu Habib,' Nick said.

'What? How the hell did that happen?' Drake thundered.

'Four men broke into the safe house to rescue him. They're all dead. And so are the MI5 agents who turned up. It's been horrific, boss,' Nick said, realising that his voice was going a little. The events of the last few hours had been overwhelming, and he had been shot.

'Oh my God!' Drake went silent for a few seconds. 'You had a young uniform officer with you?'

'PC Garrow. He's sitting next to me, driving. I got shot,' Nick said.

'Are you okay?' Drake asked.

'I'm alive. And that seems like a miracle, to be honest,' Nick admitted.

'I've sent two armed units over towards Betws-y-Coed. I'll scramble the helicopter from Conway ... What's Habib driving?' Drake asked.

'I gave the details to the receptionist so I assume they're with the CAD operator already, boss,' Nick said.

'Good,' Drake said. 'Was Ruth okay before Habib took her?'

'Yeah, she was okay. We've been through a lot tonight, boss. To complicate matters more, not only was Habib an undercover police officer working for the North West Counterterrorism Unit, it transpires that he was in reality working for a terrorist network.'

'You've lost me,' Drake said.

'He's a double agent. He made it clear that wherever he is heading tonight, he fully expects to be smuggled out of the country. He said he would be in North Africa by tomorrow,' Nick said.

'Why take Ruth?' Drake asked.

'As an insurance policy. He didn't want us running him off the road or riddling the van with bullets,' Nick explained. He wondered if he should try to ring her mobile – she had clearly had access to it.

'Getting Ruth back safely is our number one priority,' Drake said, 'But with everything that Habib knows, he must not be allowed to leave the country alive.'

CHAPTER 29

8.41 pm

IF RUTH LEANT FORWARD, she could just about see where her mobile phone rested under the driver's seat – there was no way of getting it back.

She heard Abu mutter angrily under his breath as he slowed the van down. There was a temporary traffic light that had cut the road down to one lane. A couple of workmen in orange high-vis jackets were beside the light having a chat. As the cars and lorries came the other way, Abu had no choice but to come to a halt. Ruth watched as he glanced around nervously.

Ruth could see that it would be impossible to signal to anyone from where she was sitting. She was completely trapped. She also had no idea of what Abu had in store for her when they got to wherever they were going. But given the fact that his rescuers had shot Yasir in cold blood, and he himself seemed quite prepared to kill five innocent people about twenty minutes earlier, she didn't think that he was going to let her live.

As the lights changed and the van pulled away, Ruth was jerked backwards into her seat. By her calculations, she thought that they had been stopped for well over five minutes. If Drake had heard her conversation when she dialled her phone, then those five minutes might have helped.

Pulling at the rope around her wrists, she pushed her arms together to create some slack. Then she used her fingers to feel where the knots were. Could she use a fingernail to unpick them?

'Where are we going, Abu?' Ruth asked. She wanted to distract him while she tried to loosen the ropes.

'I told you earlier to be quiet,' Abu barked.

Slowing down again, the van turned left off the main road and began to make its way down an uneven track.

'What's down here?' Ruth asked, but Abu ignored her.

Glancing out of the passenger door, Ruth got her answer. A sign read *Gwydir Airfield*.

They were flying Abu out of the country.

Suddenly, there was a deep thudding noise from above. It got louder and louder as a light washed across the road. Then the sound and light went as quickly as it had arrived.

Abu looked confused as he slowed the van and looked up.

Ruth smiled to herself. It was a helicopter.

CHAPTER 30

8.46 pm

AS PC GARROW CAME HAMMERING down a long hill, Nick saw the roadworks and solitary traffic light as they approached. There were a few workmen in orange high-vis jackets. Looking at the traffic that was backed up the other side, Nick was thankful they had caught the light on green and were able to go straight through.

'Timed that well,' PC Garrow said.

Nick wondered whether Abu and Ruth had got caught up in the roadworks. If they had, it might have slowed them down by a few crucial minutes.

His phone rang. It was Drake.

'Nick?'

'Boss?' Nick replied.

'Any visual yet?'

'Not yet,' Nick said as he scanned the traffic ahead.

Drake went silent for a few seconds. Nick could hear the sound of the control room in the background. Drake came back on the line. 'Okay, we now have a visual on the van. It's on a track that leads left off the A-four-seven-zero towards Gwydir Airfield. We have an Armed Response team about ten minutes away from there.'

'Gwydir Airfield? I know where that is, boss,' Nick said. 'I'll call when we see them.'

Nick looked over at PC Garrow and then gestured. 'Right, Jim, it's just up this hill, where that sign is.'

A few seconds later, they had reached the sign for Gwydir Airfield and turned left. They sped along the uneven track. Nick was bouncing up and down with each bump. An agonising lightning strike of pain struck his shoulder every time he was slammed back into his seat – the suspension in the van wasn't up to much.

The track was pitch black except for their headlights.

Where are they?

Suddenly, Nick saw the red glow of lights ahead. But even before he saw the number plate, he knew it was the van with Habib and Ruth inside.

'There!' Nick said.

PC Garrow slowed a little, but then spotted that the van was speeding up. 'How far up here is the airfield, sir?'

'Oh God!' Nick winced as another rut caused the van to bounce and jump. 'About a mile,' Nick said, trying to remember the tandem skydive he had done for charity a few years ago.

As they careered around a bend, the road surface got even worse.

'You think they're flying Habib out of the country from here?' PC Garrow asked.

'Not if we have anything to do with it.' Abu Habib, or whatever his real name was, needed to be brought to justice – not leave Britain to be greeted as a hero.

Despite the tight bends of the track, PC Garrow had been able to gain a bit of ground – they were now only about twenty yards behind the van.

'Easy does it,' Nick said. Ruth was inside and he wanted to rescue her in one piece.

Reaching into his waistband, Nick pulled out the Glock. He checked the magazine and then took the safety catch off.

Habib was throwing the van around every bend and braking hard, driving like a maniac.

He's going to lose control in a minute, Nick thought.

As the track straightened out, Nick looked left and saw the long expanse of the airfield. It was lit up with mini floodlights like a football stadium.

'Someone's flying in tonight,' Nick said.

He could make out the thin grey runway that ran down the middle. Dotted along the perimeter fence was an assortment of private planes of all shapes and sizes.

'Boss!' PC Garrow said urgently.

Nick looked up and saw a small red plane coming in to land. From where they were, it looked slow and graceful as it held a few feet above the tarmac before touching down.

'You think that's Habib's lift?' PC Garrow asked.

'I think it's very likely,' Nick said.

In front, the van was slaloming left and right. Then the van turned sharply, taking the corner too quickly, and the wheels lost traction on the muddy ground. Abu must have spotted the plane and taken his eyes off the track. He was trying to take back control, but Nick watched in horror as the van bounced, hit a dip, and took off. Time hung as the van flipped, almost in slow motion, like in those bad action movies, until it crashed to the ground onto its side.

Both PC Garrow and Nick shouted, '*No!*'

As the van continued to skid, it hit the perimeter fence, smashing the chain-link fencing and poles into the air.

PC Garrow hit the brakes hard and turned off the track towards where the van had slid to a stop.

Nick had no idea if Ruth was all right.

Jumping out of the van, Nick spotted the passenger door opening. Abu appeared and began to climb out.

Nick and PC Garrow sprinted towards the van. Abu jumped down, turned, and began to run across the airfield towards the red plane that was now stationary. It had to be a good three or even four hundred yards away.

Raising the gun, Nick took aim at the figure running from him. Habib was unarmed and fleeing. Was Nick really going to shoot him? There would be an enquiry. He would lose his job. They were running so fast, and Nick's arms training so rusty that if he aimed for Abu's leg, there was no guarantee he would bring him down safely or alive. What was the right thing to do?

Putting down the gun, Nick ran and jumped up on the van. He took the handle of the side door and pulled it. It was jammed.

'Jim, help me with this!' Nick shouted as PC Garrow climbed up to join him.

They pulled again. Nothing.

'Sir!' PC Garrow gestured to a small engine fire at the front of the van.

'Shit! Help me try this again,' Nick said.

With an almighty yank, they pulled the sliding side door and it rolled back.

Inside, Nick could see that Ruth was just about conscious – she had a nasty cut on her forehead and blood trickled across her face.

Thank God she's alive!

Crawling into the van, Nick looked over at the disappearing figure of Habib as he ran closer and closer to the plane.

'I'm okay here. Go after that bastard,' Nick said to PC Garrow, and then handed him the Glock. 'Ever used one of these?'

'No, sir,' PC Garrow said anxiously.

'It's just like PlayStation, just a bit heavier and more recoil. But it's just for protection – *don't* shoot him,' Nick said.

PC Garrow jumped down and disappeared.

'Any danger of you getting me out here?' Ruth mumbled.

Nick clambered down to where Ruth was tied to the seat – she was virtually upside down because of the crash.

'I think I've broken my arm,' she said.

'I'll have you out of here in a second. Promise,' Nick reassured her.

He glanced up and saw that the bonnet of the van was now on fire, flames licking the windscreen.

And he could smell petrol.

Shit! We're going to go up like a bonfire!

Fumbling with the ropes, Nick squinted as he tried to undo the knots.

'I thought you used to be a Scout,' Ruth said.

'Yeah, well I was always off having a fag in the woods when we did knots,' Nick quipped.

'Why doesn't that surprise me?' Ruth said.

Nick was now really panicking. The knots just weren't undoing – they were too thick and too tight.

'Take your time, I'm in no hurry,' Ruth said.

Nick looked at her and she smiled.

'I need to cut them with something or you're going nowhere,' Nick said.

'Oh, by the way, the engine's on fire and by the smell of it, the petrol tank and fuel line are cracked,' Ruth said very calmly.

'The glass is always half empty with you, isn't it?' Nick said as he frantically searched the van.

'I guess. I just don't fancy being the first tandoori detective,' Ruth joked.

Whoosh!

The front seats were now engulfed in flames.

Feeling the intense heat on his face, Nick looked back at Ruth – it would only be a matter of seconds before the van exploded.

Ruth was smiling, but her eyes said everything: she thought she was going to die.

'Go, Nick!' Ruth said as she coughed on the smoke.

'Go where?' Nick desperately looked around the van for something, anything, to cut through the ropes.

'Don't be a twat. You've got a wife and new baby to go to,' Ruth spluttered. 'They're going to need you. Get out now!'

'I'm not leaving you,' Nick said, shielding his face from the flames. He spotted a large plastic tub full of camping cooking equipment.

'Nick, I'm serious. That's an order,' Ruth said.

'Sorry, I can't hear you. It's a bit noisy in here.' He scrambled across the van and yanked open the lid. Tossing out pans, plates and all sorts. Right at the bottom: a large serrated knife.

Thank fuck for that!

Launching himself, Nick grabbed and cut at the rope with everything he had. He could hardly breathe now.

Whoosh!

The whole front of the van was now on fire.

Blinking, Nick could hardly see in the smoke and heat. The sweat dripped down his face, but it was so hot it almost evaporated straight away.

Suddenly, the ropes fell away and Ruth pulled her arms free.

Grabbing her hands, Nick pulled her with the last remains of his strength towards the open sliding door above them.

She slipped. Nick was anxious she'd fall back and out of his reach.

With both hands, Nick pulled Ruth as she clambered out and they both jumped down and onto the grass.

'Come on!' Nick shouted as he yanked Ruth backwards and away from the burning van.

'Jim?' Ruth gasped as they ran.

Taking a few steps to one side, Nick and Ruth could see that Habib had now reached the small red plane. The door over the wing opened.

PC Garrow was running, but he was a good fifty yards behind.

'Jim's not going to get there in time,' Ruth said.

'And that bastard is going to get away,' Nick said.

Abu was reaching up to climb into the body of the plane when—

Crack! Crack! Crack!

Even though it was in the distance, Nick knew that sound – he'd been hearing it all night. Gunfire.

What the hell is going on?

Abu Habib's body froze and fell backwards onto the ground.

He's been shot.

'What's going on?' Ruth said.

PC Garrow stopped running now.

The wing door closed, and the plane began to taxi around and away.

'They shot him?' Nick said.

'What? They've killed him?' Ruth said.

'After all that, they just shot him because he was a liability!' Nick growled.

For a few seconds, Ruth and Nick stood quietly looking over the airfield.

'Thanks for that,' Ruth said.

'Thanks for what?' He knew what she meant.

'For saving my life.'

'Oh, that.' Nick turned to look at the blazing van. 'Well, as long as it's put you off smoking, you're welcome.'

'I wouldn't go that far,' Ruth said with a smile.

'I need to find a phone and ring Amanda,' Nick said as he took a few steps away from Ruth.

'I can't wait to hear what you're going to say when she asks how your day's been,' Ruth said as she started to cough again.

Nick turned, smiled and began to walk away.

'Oh, she's going to be so piss—'

BANG!

The flaming remains of the van exploded, sending a fireball up into the sky.

Nick felt himself being lifted off his feet, into the air ... and then everything went black.

CHAPTER 31

IT WAS NEARLY MIDNIGHT by the time Ruth pulled up outside Sian's brother's house in a small cul-de-sac in Llancastell. An X-ray had shown that her right arm was only sprained, not broken, but it was still in a sling, and she had been given strong painkillers. That was the beauty of an automatic car, Ruth thought. You can drive it with one hand.

Buzzing down the window, Ruth let the cold autumnal breeze blow into the car. The residential close was dark, quiet and still. She soaked up the peace and tranquillity for a few seconds. It was impossible to process what had happened that day. What she should have done was gone home, had a hot bath and a stiff drink, taken a few painkillers, and slept. Tomorrow was going to be a very long day. A series of meetings and debriefings with Drake, Special Branch, and the Security Service. She would have to talk to the media desk and keep officers in CID up to speed.

Ruth gazed over at the house. Was it selfish to knock on the door this late? Probably. And even though the events of the day were now national news, Ruth hadn't heard from Sian. Ruth had sent her a text from Llancastell Hospital to say that she was okay, but received no response.

However, Ruth knew she needed to see Sian. It was a compulsion. But it didn't make any sense. If she wanted to see Sian this desperately, why had Ruth lied to her and treated her so badly? Was she one of those people who only wanted to be with someone when they were gone? Was it just too easy when Sian had been her partner?

Grabbing a bottle of their favourite white wine from the passenger seat, Ruth got out of the car. She slammed the car door, and it seemed to reverberate around the whole close. It was that quiet.

She walked up to the front door, knocked gently and waited. After about thirty seconds, the door unlocked and then opened a little.

When Sian saw it was Ruth, her eyes widened. 'Oh my God! Are you okay? I've been watching the news.'

Ruth nodded. 'Yeah, I'm okay.'

'Jesus. I can't believe you got caught up in all that.'

'Yeah. I should probably be dead,' Ruth answered, well aware that she was trying to make Sian feel guilty. She should have felt bad, but she didn't have the energy.

'Thank God, you're not.'

There were a few seconds as they looked at each other.

Are you glad because you still love me? Is that what you mean? Ruth thought with a nervous sense of hope.

'I brought wine,' Ruth said, lifting up the bottle.

'I can see that.'

'I did text you from the hospital,' Ruth said.

Ruth looked at Sian for any sign or hint that she still loved her.

'I know.' Sian locked eyes with Ruth. Her expression cooled. 'What are you doing here, Ruth?'

'I wanted to see you,' Ruth said.

There was no hesitation. 'I don't want to see you. I'm glad you're okay, but I just can't. You know how I feel about us, so I don't know why you're here on my doorstep,' Sian said.

'Can't I come in? Just for a glass of wine?' Ruth asked.

'Why? I just don't think that's a good idea,' Sian said, her eyes glassy with tears.

'After today, I just ...' Ruth wasn't quite sure how to finish the sentence.

'I'm sorry you've had a horrendous day, but it doesn't change anything. It doesn't mean that I now trust you any more than I did. It doesn't mean that you can put your past behind you and move on. None of that has suddenly changed, has it?' Sian's countenance swayed between emotional tears and bubbling annoyance.

'No ... I'm sorry,' Ruth said. She could see Sian was upset and didn't know what else to say.

What the hell am I doing?

'I just need you to go, okay?' Sian said as she slowly closed the door.

Ruth took a breath, turned, and headed back to the car.

NICK WAS SLOWLY BECOMING aware of a beeping sound as he drifted in and out of consciousness. Then the mumble of voices. Someone took his hand and checked his pulse.

His eyelids felt heavy and limbs like lead. Blinking, Nick tried to open his eyes.

'Hello, love,' said a familiar female voice. *Auntie Pat?*

Trying to move up in the bed, a nurse came over. 'Try not to move too much at the moment, Nick.'

Managing to lift both eyes open now, Nick tried to remember what was going on. Where was he? What day was it? The last thing he remembered was getting Ruth out of the van, but then nothing.

'Where am I?' Nick said, trying to focus on the room. His voice was croaky – he needed water.

'You're in Llancastell Hospital. But you're going to be fine,' Auntie Pat said.

As he focussed, Nick saw his aunt's face decorated with a warm smile as he had done so many times as a boy.

Then Nick felt a surge of panic. 'What about Amanda? The baby? What's happened?'

Auntie Pat reached over and touched his hand. 'Don't worry. The baby's fine.'

Nick felt like he'd been punched hard in the gut. He'd missed it. He'd missed the birth of his child. 'She's had the baby?' his voice swaying between elation, disappointment and exhaustion.

A male voice came from the other side of the bed. 'You had a baby girl. Six pounds, five ounces. About six o'clock this morning.'

It was Tony. He was sitting in a wheelchair and smiling at him.

'Have you seen her?' Nick asked.

'Yes, she's beautiful,' Tony replied, nodding.

A nurse came in holding a baby in a white blanket. 'Would you like to meet your daughter, Mr Evans?'

The nurse approached, turned the baby, and then laid his daughter across his chest. He took her in his arms and looked at her face. Her tiny nose, blinking eyes, and perfect skin.

'Oh my God. She is beautiful ... Hello, hello, little one,' Nick said, with tears coming to his eyes. 'Is Amanda resting?' He looked to the adults.

As eyes darted around the room, there was a palpable silence. Nick's stomach turned.

'What's the matter?' Nick asked as he was filled with panic.

The nurse looked at him. 'Amanda had a haemorrhage during the birth. She lost a lot of blood and her blood pressure dropped.'

Nick couldn't believe what he was hearing. 'But she's going to be okay?'

'She's stable at the moment. And she's getting the best care that we can give her,' the nurse said with a kind smile.

However, something about the nurse's lack of certainty or reassurance made the bottom fall out of Nick's world.

CHAPTER 32

DRAKE HAD TOLD RUTH to take the day off, but she couldn't rest. She had gone to work just to keep busy, which worked as the day was spent in endless meetings, debriefs and phone calls. Finally, after two hours with Drake, Special Branch, MI5, and the chief constable of North Wales Police, she was ordered to go home.

Having rung the hospital to check on Nick's progress, she decided she might visit him the next morning. Despite various phone calls, she couldn't seem to get much more information than Amanda had given birth to a healthy baby girl, but that she had lost a lot of blood and had been taken to the ICU as a precaution.

As she pottered around the kitchen, finding any house-work jobs she could think of to amuse her, she could see that it was only 4 pm. What to do now? How to fill the empty hours? Opening a new bottle of red wine, she poured herself a large glass of Merlot. She needed to change the way she felt, or at least numb the shock and pain of the past twenty-four hours.

Wandering into the living room, she flicked through the CDs. When Sian had lived there, they had always used Spotify, but Ruth had no idea how to use that or play music from her phone. She spotted a copy of a James Bay album - *Chaos and the Calm.* It was Sian's. She must have left it here.

Picking it up, Ruth looked at the cover and then at the track listing on the back. There had been a few months where they had played the CD to death. She put it on and selected the song 'Scars'.

With tears in her eyes, Ruth took a breath, finished the glass of wine in two large gulps, and went to the kitchen. She poured another large glass, took her cigarettes from the counter, and began to walk towards the garden. But she stopped.

Fuck it! If I live on my own, I can smoke in my own fucking house.

She returned to the counter, knocked a cigarette out of the box with one hand, and lit it.

As she went back into the living room, she had an idea. Sian had made her feelings clear last night – hence drowning her sorrows in wine – so there was nothing stopping her from delving into the past anymore. She needed a distraction, and uncovering what she could about Sarah's disappearance, now that they finally had a lead, would do just that. Grabbing the laptop, she opened it and went onto Google. She searched 'Secret Garden sex parties'. The elite events company was run by Jamie Parsons, who said he had first met Sarah there. He went on to introduce Sarah to Jurgen Kessler, who was a friend of his from business school.

A homepage flashed up with a woman and man wearing black eye masks in a sexy embrace.

Ruth picked up her phone and dialled.

After a few rings, a woman's voice answered. 'Hello, Secret Garden?'

Ruth took a breath and then said, 'I wonder if you can tell me how I can order a ticket for one of your parties?'

NICK HAD DRIFTED IN and out of sleep for hours but still felt tired. He was on strong pain medication, antibiotics, and a saline drip. Despite regular requests, he had had no news of Amanda except that she had been operated on and was in recovery.

As he forced his eyes open, he saw Auntie Pat asleep in the armchair beside him, but Tony was gone. He was probably with Amanda, or at least finding out how she was. Nick tried to sit up. It was agony. He felt like he had been run over by a lorry – and then reversed over again. Every part of his body seemed to ache or spasm with pain.

Glancing up at the clock on the wall, it was five thirty in the afternoon. The last time he had looked was at midday. He had been out of it for most of the day.

Where the hell is Amanda? What was going on? Nick's pulse began to race as his anxiety increased. He tried to console himself that if anything awful had happened he would have heard something by now. Wouldn't he? He didn't even want to think about it. He wouldn't let his mind entertain any thoughts that something had gone horribly wrong.

Lying in his hospital bed, Nick tried to process what had happened over the past twenty-four hours. It had been like being in a Jack Reacher book; things like that just didn't happen in North Wales. He thought of the MI5 officers, Adam Cavendish and Sophie Greene. It was so tragic that they had lost their lives last night. If there was any tiny consolation, it was that the men who had come to rescue Abu Habib had died, and so eventually had Habib himself. It wasn't justice, but it would have to do.

Taking the remote control in his left hand, Nick looked up at the television on the wall. Maybe he could watch something to distract himself? A sitcom?

The door to his single room began to open slowly. Nick glanced over. He hoped it was someone with news of Amanda.

A figure hobbled in with the aid of stick. Tony. He looked over but didn't say anything. A nurse followed, glanced over at Nick and then came towards him.

Nick was desperately trying to read her expression. Was she there to tell him some terrible news or not?

Please God, let this be good news.

Nick dared not breathe.

'Nick?' the nurse said very gently.

'Yes,' Nick said – he couldn't get out any more words. He was starting to feel very shaky.

'I wondered if you were up for a couple of visitors,' the nurse said with a smile.

As Nick glanced over, he saw that Tony was still holding the door wide open.

Still not exactly certain about what the nurse meant, Nick nodded, 'Erm ... Sure ...'

Almost as if in slow motion, the spokes of a wheel from a wheelchair appeared from behind the door.

And then Nick took a breath as his heart leapt.

Sitting in the wheelchair was Amanda, wrapped in a blanket. She had their baby cradled in her arms.

Amanda smiled over at him. He could see she looked exhausted and pale.

'Hello, Daddy,' Amanda said as their eyes met.

Enjoy this book?
Get the next book in the series

Publication date November 2020
The Solace Farm Killings
A Ruth Hunter Crime Thriller #Book 7

Your FREE book is waiting for you now

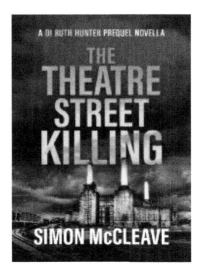

Get your FREE copy of the prequel to
the DI Ruth Hunter Series NOW
at www.simonmccleave.com[1]
and join my VIP Email Club

---

1. http://www.simonmccleave.com

Printed in Great Britain
by Amazon

41933180R00138